"Admit it, Cassandra. Long ago and far away, you and I once made a baby."

Cassie's eyes were bleak, wary, frightened, when she finally looked up. "Maybe that's true, but he's mine now," she whispered to Gray. "Rob's a happy, carefree little boy. He's not built to be one of the lofty, rule-the-world Alexanders, and I won't risk having him hurt by trying to make him fit in your world," she insisted.

"I'm going—for now. But understand that I'll be back, Cassie. He's my son, too, and I won't allow any more time to pass before I claim him."

She looked up at Gray, her arms still tightly clutching herself as he climbed into his car.

"Two days," he said simply. "I'll give you two days to tell him, and then I'll expect to meet my son, come hell or high water."

Dear Reader,

This April, Silhouette Romance showers you with six spectacular stories from six splendid authors! First, our exciting LOVING THE BOSS miniseries continues as rising star Robin Wells tells the tale of a demure accountant who turns daring to land her boss—and become mommy to *The Executive's Baby.*

Prince Charming's Return signals Myrna Mackenzie's return to Silhouette Romance. In this modern-day fairy-tale romance, wealthy FABULOUS FATHER Gray Alexander discovers he has a son, but the proud mother of his child refuses marriage—unless love enters the equation.... Sandra Steffen's BACHELOR GULCH miniseries is back with *Wes Stryker's Wrangled Wife!* In this spirited story, a pretty stranger just passing through town can't resist a sexy cowboy struggling to raise two orphaned tykes.

Cara Colter revisits the lineup with *Truly Daddy,* an emotional, heartwarming novel about a man who learns what it takes to be a father—and a husband—through the transforming love of a younger woman. When *A Cowboy Comes a Courting* in Christine Scott's contribution to HE'S MY HERO!, the virginal heroine who'd sworn off sexy, stubborn, Stetson-wearing rodeo stars suddenly finds herself falling hopelessly in love. And FAMILY MATTERS showcases Patti Standard's newest novel in which a man with a knack for fixing things sets out to make a struggling single mom and her teenage daughter *His Perfect Family.*

As always, I hope you enjoy this month's offerings, and the wonderful ones still to come!

Happy reading!

Mary-Theresa Hussey

Mary-Theresa Hussey
Senior Editor, Silhouette Romance

Please address questions and book requests to:
Silhouette Reader Service
U.S.: 3010 Walden Ave., P.O. Box 1325, Buffalo, NY 14269
Canadian: P.O. Box 609, Fort Erie, Ont. L2A 5X3

PRINCE CHARMING'S RETURN

Myrna Mackenzie

To my father-in-law, Dr. Harold Topol,
my unofficial public relations director.
Thank you for being so supportive.

SILHOUETTE BOOKS

ISBN 0-373-19361-0

PRINCE CHARMING'S RETURN

This edition published by arrangement with Harlequin Books S.A.

Printed in U.S.A.

Books by Myrna Mackenzie

Silhouette Romance

The Baby Wish #1046
The Daddy List #1090
Babies and a Blue-Eyed Man #1182
The Secret Groom #1225
The Scandalous Return of Jake Walker #1256
Prince Charming's Return #1361

MYRNA MACKENZIE,

winner of the Holt Medallion Award honoring outstanding literary talent, has always been fascinated by the belief that within every man is a hero, inside every woman lives a heroine. She loves to write about ordinary people making extraordinary dreams come true. A former teacher, Myrna lives in the suburbs of Chicago with her husband—who was her high school sweetheart—and her two sons. She believes in love, laughter, music, vacations to the mountains, watching the stars, anything unattached to the words *physical fitness* and letting dust balls gather where they may. Readers can write to Myrna at P.O. Box 225, LaGrange, IL 60525-0225.

From the Journal of Grayson Alexander

Something happened last night, and my life is going to change. It's been eleven years since I've seen Cassandra Pratt. We never really knew each other—but one day when I was nineteen and home from college, I ran into her and...things happened.

It seemed like magic at first. We ended up making love, but the magic must have been one-sided, because she didn't want to see me after that. Two months later, I heard that she and Jake Walker had left town, and eventually Cass had a baby.

Up until yesterday, I thought—everyone thought—the baby was Jake's and that he'd deserted her. But he came back to town, and my ex-fiancée, Tess, fell in love with him and decided to clear his name. So last night, Tess stood up at a public meeting and made an announcement. It seems Jake Walker doesn't have a child. I do. And whether she likes it or not, I'm going to call on Cassandra Pratt today. To claim my son. Cass and I are going to get to know each other. ***Out*** *of bed this time.*

Prologue

Stay away from Gray or, believe me, I'll put you and your parents right out on the street. Hugh Alexander's warning rumbled through Cassandra Pratt's mind even as her shaky legs carried her near the university lecture hall where Gray, Hugh's son, was attending classes.

"Don't think, just don't think," she whispered out loud.

No way should she be here. At seventeen, she was a year too young to be on campus. And worse, there was Mr. Alexander's all too real and frightening threat. She'd obeyed him for two months, but…

Cassie curved her palm gently against her abdomen, seeking out the life still known only to herself. Closing her eyes, she blocked the sight of the wealthy young college students so different from herself and tried to concentrate on finding the man she'd come to see.

"Gray." Her voice was hushed. She'd lived her life dreaming of him, a girl from the muddy side of town watching and wishing from afar. And then one day, his last day of spring break, their paths had accidentally crossed; he'd been kind. For one day and night she'd lived her fairy tale, only to lose it the next day when Hugh Alexander had pounded on her door.

Gray's got plenty of female toys, Hugh Alexander had said. *I don't want him linked with the daughter of a leech and a drunk. He's an Alexander.* And as an Alexander in the town of Misunderstood, Hugh could make her family suffer. His family owned a large chunk of the town. There was more than one business bearing the Alexander name.

"Don't worry, I'm here," she whispered to her child just as the door to the lecture hall opened. And suddenly Gray was there, too, with his chestnut hair, his long-legged stride. Her heart lurched. She raised a hand to signal from the trees where she was standing.

"Gray! Over here."

The female voice snagged Cassie's attention. Gray smiled at the beautiful, young blonde walking toward him. A girl whose clothes were richly made.

And reality returned, full force. Cassie ran one palm over her own threadbare jeans, jeans that would be too snug to wear in the not-too-distant future.

"Sheila," Gray said, waving at the girl. "What are you doing here?"

Words that might easily have been meant for herself, Cassie acknowledged. What on earth was *she* doing here?

Pain and panic buffeted her as she watched the two clearly matched young people standing before her. She should have run that night. Instead she'd gloried in Gray's voice, his scent, his gentle touch. It was only the next time he'd called that she'd turned him away. She'd followed Hugh Alexander's orders, and it was clear now that he had been right. About the other women.

"I was worried when you didn't come for coffee this morning with everyone else," the girl said, her voice smooth and refined. "Studying again, I'll bet. Don't you ever rest?"

Gray's answering half smile reminded Cass of how he'd

looked braced above her, just before he'd kissed her, before he'd sent the world spinning away. She sucked in her breath.

"I was talking with Professor Grant. About the family businesses, my plans, the responsibility I have to my hometown, the Alexander name and...hey, don't look so pained. It's what I've always wanted to do, what I was raised for."

"And no time for life? Fun? Love?"

"Not love," he said suddenly, then blew out a breath. "I'm sorry, Sheila, but that's just not for me."

She wrinkled her pretty nose. "So you'll uphold the family name by becoming the last Alexander?"

A chuckle escaped Gray, low and husky and mesmerizing. "I never said I wasn't going to marry, but that's a long ways away. And it won't be a marriage based on love."

But it would be a marriage with the kind of woman that would be a credit to the Alexander name, Cassie thought, trying to ignore the ache that welled up inside her.

And when Gray heard the secret she'd come to tell him? What would he say then, he who *was* a man who believed in responsibility? When he heard the news, his sense of duty would war with his plans, but...he might insist on doing the right thing. *She could be with him.*

And she would always know why he had stayed, Cass admitted. As her mother had always known about her father.

Gray could hate her and her child, the way her father hated her mother—and her.

But how could she not tell him? She had to, didn't she?

Cassie held her breath as Gray looked down at the girl, brushing her nose with his finger. "Come on. Enough talk about me. I'll buy you lunch."

The lovely girl stared up at him, wide-eyed, worshipful, the way Cassie knew she herself had often watched Gray.

Only this young woman was the right kind, not a Pratt—and she was moving away with Gray.

Step out from the trees, Cass ordered herself. *You have to tell him. Now.*

But watching them leaving together, she couldn't move, couldn't squeeze the words out. She wondered if the girl was just the friend she appeared to be or if she was his someday wife. She wondered if the girl knew about her, about Cassie Pratt.

Of course she didn't. There was nothing to tell.

Just one night when Cassie had practically begged a boy to make love to her. A nineteen-year-old boy whose life had been planned from birth.

Longing to run now, she forced herself forward.

But she saw the girl bump slightly against Gray, saw how he reached out to gently steady her, naturally, as if they'd shared such moments and others a thousand times before.

And Cassie backed away, swiftly, nearly stumbling.

If she followed, she would have to explain why she was here, and that would change everyone's lives. It could be terrible. For her. For him. But most of all, for the child. Her child might become a duty—or an embarrassment. Unwanted and resented. But the one thing her child would never become, she was sure now, was the loving offspring of a happily married couple named Gray and Cassandra.

It was what she had hoped, Cassie realized. Up until this minute she'd still been clinging to the dream. Foolishly. For of course, if Gray decided to take responsibility for his child, no happiness would come out of such a situation. She knew. Her own world had been built on just such a mistake.

"Don't worry," she whispered to the child who had to come first. "I'll take care of you. Always. Together we'll make our own dreams."

And pressing her fingers to her lips, Cassie turned and fled. She ran from her heart, from her fears, from the boy she couldn't help wanting...and from the dream she should never have dreamed in the first place.

Chapter One

"Okay, Cass, you sweet-lipped liar. I'd say it's way past time you and I came face-to-face. Again."

Gray Alexander whispered the words as he pulled off the cherry-orchard-flanked road that led to this country store, this house. The woman before him was bent over a bucket of soapy water, standing next to a partially washed green rust bucket of a car drying in the late July heat. Soapsuds sluiced down her bare legs, there were damp spots on her red T-shirt and frayed cutoffs, and her midnight hair was pulled back in an unruly braid. As she straightened, more strands escaped, the thick, loose curls kissing her neck and clinging to her moist skin. She was a mess. Slippery. Unkempt. Still absolutely stunning, Gray conceded as he edged his car closer.

"Hell," Gray murmured, registering that unwelcome thought.

It had been eleven years since he had last seen Cass. She was already in her late twenties, but it was absolutely clear that Mother Nature had only improved on a good thing. It was also clear that the lady hadn't yet realized that the car pulling into her driveway belonged to him. Good. He wanted to be close enough to see her reaction when she realized that the truth was finally out, that the piper had come for payment in full. He and Cassie Pratt were about to do battle, and he intended to win.

The crunch and grumble of gravel under almost two tons of metal quieted as he threw the Lexus into Park and climbed out.

Cassie stood silently, her sponge dripping suds on the ground as she watched him approach. A limp-eared, sad-eyed giant of a mutt sat beside her, whimpering and thumping his tail against the ground, practically knocking her over with his wriggling body. Eyeing Gray, she reached down and ran soothing fingers over the dog's head.

"It's all right, Bailey." Her whispered words were meant to reassure the animal, but her eyes were wary and watchful. "Gray?" she asked as if she wasn't sure that he was a real, in-the-flesh male and not just some ghost come to haunt her.

"Gray," he agreed. "Been a hell of a long time, hasn't it, Cass? Last time I called you, I recall you saying that it was best if we didn't see each other anymore," he said, twisting his lips up in a grimace. "But times change. And circumstances change sometimes, too, now don't they?"

He took a step closer.

She started to step back, then held her ground.

Gray felt a grudging respect, but that didn't change things. When the truth had come crashing down upon him yesterday, he'd been overcome with shock and guilt—but that had been yesterday. Today he felt the anger, the injustice, the terrible sense of loss. He had found out at thirty what he should have been told at nineteen, and right now he wanted nothing more than to shake Cass until she spilled her secrets, to demand she give him back what she had taken from him.

But, of course, he would do neither of those things. Alexander men didn't use physical force, especially not on women. They simply lived up to their responsibilities, and he fully intended to do that. Otherwise he wouldn't be here. Not in ten thousand lifetimes. The last thing he wanted to do was stir the ashes of the past, but he was going to do that. Right now.

Gray took one more step nearer. He moved forward into Cassie's space, and those blue eyes widened with instant alarm.

"What are you doing here, Gray? Why now? There's nothing much down this road but Michigan cherry orchards and me, and you're a good seventy-five miles from home." Cassie's voice was low, the slightest thread of sound.

Gray tilted his head. "I'm not here by accident, if that's what you mean, Cass. It's definitely you that I came to see. And by the way, in case you're worried, don't be." He nodded toward where her fingers had curled deeply into her dog's fur. "I've learned to keep my hands to myself over the years."

She stiffened suddenly, sucked in an audible breath. A wave of dusty rose climbed up her throat. But she lifted her fingers from Bailey's furry head and waved the dog away. Freed from his meager guard duties, her pet trotted off to nose among the flowers. Cassie watched him go. She rested her free hand on the slick metal of her car. "All right," she said slowly, her voice a cool, unwelcoming curl of sound. "You've come to see me. Tell me why."

God, he almost had to admire her. She was clearly nervous. He could see the panicked pounding of her pulse in her throat, but she was going to guts it out, to pretend bravery and innocence. Hell, if he didn't resent her so much, he could almost applaud the lady.

"Maybe I just want to talk about old times," he drawled.

"I don't believe in nostalgia," she whispered. "The past is unimportant."

"Depends on which part of the past we're discussing, doesn't it, Cass?"

She stared at him, her wide sapphire eyes filled with...sadness? No, of course not. She'd known the damage she was doing. Why be sad? He was just seeing what he wanted to see. No way was the lady sorry. She'd had eleven years to put things to rights.

"Gray," she began, her voice breaking.

She stopped, took a breath, raised her chin higher. "I'm sorry, Gray, but I really should get back to the store." She started to turn.

He almost reached out and grabbed for her hand. The thought of touching her, of sliding his fingers against her own held a certain appeal. Damn. Just curiosity, he told himself. Just wondering if the smoke they'd created all those years ago had simply been a fluke of chemistry based on youth and hormones and the recurring insanity of spring.

Stupid thought. Nonsense. Of course he wouldn't do that. He wouldn't touch her, didn't want to touch her, and besides, it wasn't his style to hold a woman by force. But she was still moving away and he had to change her mind. Fortunately he had other ammo.

"This concerns Jake Walker," he said, keeping his voice low and speculative. "The man was once a friend of yours, wasn't he?"

Cassie stopped in her tracks, still as a tree in calm weather. "Jake *is* a friend of mine," she said.

Gray studied the pale, taut line of her jaw, the darkness of her lashes in comparison. "I know. I remember that you were the only real friend he had at one time, so I'm sure you already know he's back in town after being gone eleven years."

She nodded, her eyes even more wary than they had

been, if that were possible. "What do you want to know about Jake? And why?"

Tilting his head, Gray stared directly into her face. He forced himself to take the full effect of those seemingly vulnerable blue eyes. "In other words, what business is it of mine?"

"Maybe."

Funny, he remembered her as a shy little dove, but now even though her body was rigid, and she was clearly uncomfortable, she was standing her ground, practically daring him to accuse her of something.

He was willing to play the game. For a while.

"Jake came back to fix up his mother's house. I'm on the preservation committee, I've had some contact with him."

"And you want...information from me?"

He definitely wanted information, but not about the house.

"Yes," he said, watching her carefully. "I heard you had a visitor yesterday."

The wary look in Cassie's eyes melted away. The tight line of her lips softened at his words. She stepped forward, moved closer, her eyes wide with concern. "Is this about your fiancée, about Tess?" she asked. "She came here yesterday. To meet me. To ask for help. She said she'd been working with Jake and was worried he was being misjudged..."

Holding up one hand, Gray stopped her midsentence. "I know Tess came by, and frankly, I'm sure she was more than just worried. She's planning on having babies with the guy."

Bingo. His pointed barb hit home. Finally she moved back a step, but the concern in her eyes didn't lessen.

"Jake won't let anything happen between them," she finally said, squaring her shoulders. "I can promise you that, Gray. No matter what people have said about him in the past, he's an honorable man. If that's what you wanted to ask me about, I—''

''No.'' Gray moved closer, close enough to smell the soapsuds on her skin, to almost feel the warmth of her breath as she tried to convince him Jake wouldn't harm him or his.

''I'm not here to talk about how Tess and Jake feel about each other. That doesn't matter to me now.''

He shook his head at the confused look in her eyes. He'd just bet she was wondering how he could be so nonchalant about his fiancée falling for another man, but he wasn't prepared to discuss the practical nature of his relationship with Tess. Moreover, he didn't want to be sidetracked by trying to explain why he could never be a part of the type of emotion-based relationship that most people longed for. It didn't matter. There were more important things to discuss right now.

''I want to know a few things—about Jake,'' he said. ''When he left town eleven years ago, I was away at school, but you were right behind him, I was told. Everyone assumed you'd gone with him and that he'd abandoned you later.''

Cassie's blue eyes narrowed. ''Anyone who thinks that...never knew Jake.''

But Cassie had known Jake—and the man had known her. Well enough that he'd been privy to her secrets. His name had been intimately connected with hers. Gray sucked in air at the thought, remembered the unwarranted resentment he'd felt at the time. But that was over, gone. There was only one thing between him and Cassie now. One very important thing.

''You're right. I didn't know Jake,'' he agreed. ''But I thought I knew you just a little. I was wrong, but still...why didn't you tell me the truth? That Jake didn't seduce and abandon you?''

Cassie stared at him, silenced by his words. She took a

long, deep breath. "Maybe because it was never any of your concern, Gray. You and I weren't— I haven't discussed Jake with anyone until yesterday, and only then because I realized Tess was genuinely worried that people were misjudging him. Jake is my closest friend, and we both know the truth. But we've also both been gone from Misunderstood for years, and gossip like that tends to stick close to home. There didn't seem to be any point in making such a statement. Until now."

"Like hell there wouldn't have been, Cass. You know I would have been here long ago if I'd had any idea how things really were. After that day, I had a responsibility to you."

Silence followed, long and deep, so that the songs of the birds in the trees seemed suddenly too loud.

"There was no reason for you to feel that way," she finally said, her voice as quiet and calm as the weather. But her eyelids flickered for just a second. Her fingers pressed more tightly against the car. Her breath came just a touch too quickly.

"Don't give me that garbage," he said, running one hand through his hair. "Did you think once I realized you and I had unfinished business I wouldn't have taken care of things? If I didn't make it clear I was that kind of guy, then hell, I'm sorry about that, but that still doesn't change the truth."

Cassie was soldier-still, one hand on the car, the other clinging to the drying sponge. Her cheeks were glowing a dull pink, but she raised one brow in an imperious gesture. "Don't be sorry, Gray," she said quietly. "And don't be wrong. There's no reason for you to be here, ever, and I can't think of any business you and I didn't complete years ago."

Gray studied the please-leave-now look in the eyes of the woman who'd just, essentially, called him a liar. She raised her chin to meet his gaze, and the proud gesture, when she had to know her back was to the wall, won his respect if not his sympathy. He felt an irritating urge to reach out and stroke one finger down the line of her cheek, to see if he could make that stoney facade crumble, but he'd touched her before and unleashed...trouble. The worst kind of trouble. He wouldn't do that again.

Carefully he tamped down the disconcerting attraction that had caught him in its grasp once before. He backed away from it. Cassie had closed the book on him many years ago, and he had no intention of peeling back her pages ever again. What he needed from her now was information and cooperation, and from the angle of that little chin, it almost seemed like he might have made the trip for no reason at all. She was doing her best to make it look as if he had jumped to some false conclusions. Her stance was "you're dead wrong," but her movements were too controlled, her fingers clenched on the sponge just a hair too tightly.

Without thinking, he reached out and coaxed her hand open, letting the sponge fall back into the bucket.

He ignored her slight gasp as he touched her, ignored the almost imperceptible tremor that slid through her as he dragged his hand against hers. And he for damn sure forced himself to ignore the unexpected, unwanted flicker of heat that curled inside himself, as well.

Swearing beneath his breath, he released her hand, and the tips of her fingers raked across his bare palm.

Gray concentrated on his anger, forced himself to turn away from the attraction simmering just beneath the surface. It was meaningless, what any man and woman who had once known each other in the most basic way would feel if they parted and came together again. Meaningless. But other things weren't, and those things had been ignored way the hell too long.

"All right, Cass, let's stop dancing around the issue. The facts are that you didn't run away with Jake eleven years ago, and you had a child soon after that. So where's my son, Cassie?'' His voice was deadly calm as he broached the most important subject of his life, but his hands were clenched into fists and his eyes felt like two burning torches.

Cassie sucked in a long, deep breath, then froze, as if realizing that her action gave away too much. Slowly she leaned back against the damp car, crossing her ankles in a movement that was just a little too studied to be ''cool.''

''Who's been feeding you that line of hooey, Gray?''

If the situation hadn't been so serious, if he hadn't already been on his feet, Gray would have given the woman a standing ovation. Cassandra Pratt was the only child of the meanest, hardest-drinking, foul-mouthed man in five counties. Yet in a situation that clearly had her ducking for cover and hiding behind lies, that had to have her so hopping mad she could barely maintain her casual facade, the worst word she could bring herself to use was ''hooey.''

''The word on the street after your little chat with Tess yesterday, sweetheart, is that Jake Walker isn't the father of your child.''

Silence, simple and stunning, crept in.

''I never said he was,'' she said at last.

''You never said he wasn't until Tess asked you point-blank and you were forced to confess. And you *knew* what everyone thought. The entire town of Misunderstood believed Jake had fathered your child after you both were expelled for making love in that closet at the high school.''

Cassie drew her brows together. She pushed back her shoulders, narrowed her eyes. ''I don't care what everyone thought that day. Jake and I never—''

Gray *did* smile then.

''Never what, Cassie?''

His words brought her upright off the car. She crossed her arms at her chest, and her madder-than-heck gesture tightened the wet red cloth of her T-shirt against her breasts. Gray took a deep drag of air, cursed himself for being a normal, red-blooded, fire-breathing man.

Clearly oblivious to the enticing picture she represented, Cassie stared up at him. "Jake never touched me that way, and he never would have. That day...I was— I was telling Jake that I was pregnant. I guess I was...a bit overemotional. The way all women are who have hormones racing through their bodies," she declared, daring him to disagree with her.

"Jake was simply comforting me, no matter what it might have looked like. He was just being a friend," she continued, her voice softening, her eyes dark with apparent guilt. "But when the door opened and all those people came running, everyone jumped to conclusions. I was too dazed and scared to explain, Jake didn't want to explain, and what followed was a serious misunderstanding which ballooned into a bit of gossip so juicy no one could have stopped it. It's true I made things worse by leaving town soon after he did, but I had my reasons, and I explained all that nonsense about Jake to Tess just yesterday. I'm sure she must have told you the truth. You're engaged to her, after all."

"Was engaged," he corrected.

Turning her head to the side, Cassie bit her lip. "I'm sorry for that, then. It was clear Tess loved Jake when she came to ask me to help him. That's why I finally caved in and talked, even though I've always known Jake's word and mine never counted for much in Misunderstood. But—" She looked at Gray with suddenly sad eyes. "Jake's always been there for me. I wanted him to have someone else other than me who cared whether he lived or died, but I didn't think about how that would affect you, that she would leave you for Jake as a result of our conversation. I didn't know you would lose her."

"Tess didn't break off the engagement, Cass. I did."

"Because you knew that she loved him?"

Gray moved to stand in front of Cassie. He looked down at her, at the satiny braid that had slipped over one shoulder making her look almost like a child with her head tilted down that way. But she was no child. She was a woman. The woman who had knowingly stolen his son.

"Gray?"

"What happened between Tess and myself isn't important here," he said. "But I called things off mainly because you and I have unfinished business. I have responsibilities of my own to take care of, wrongs to right."

She nearly bumped against him as her body stiffened, as she suddenly raised her chin five notches.

"What...what in the world do you mean by that, Grayson Alexander?"

Whatever calm she had claimed when he'd first arrived, was nowhere to be seen now. She was ruffled, her eyes flashing diamond-blue sparks, her arms pulled tightly against her body. She was also something else. Scared? Gray ignored the tug of guilt that pulled at him. It wasn't important.

"He's my son, Cass."

"Why do you keep saying that?"

"Because it's true. You were a virgin the night we made love."

Cassie sucked in an audible breath. She looked at Gray dead-on. "You and I never made love. We had a...a one night physical experience that should never have happened in the first place."

So she was going to brazen this out to the end. Fine, he'd dealt with that attitude before. If she wanted to lie to herself, okay, but he would have the truth for himself. Gray reached out and cupped her chin, his fingers firm against her butterfly-soft skin. He held her there, immobile. No force. She was probably almost as startled as he was that he'd dared to touch her again in such an intimate way.

"Let's shoot for at least a touch of honesty here, Cass. Not long before that fabled day with Jake, I became your first lover. I was with you for one whole day and half the night, Cass. Naked. We made long, slow love. Passionately. Many times. But what's real important, the only thing that's actually important, is that you conceived a child that night. And you never let me know."

Gray could feel Cassie's pulse beneath his fingers coming faster and faster. "My son is mine," she said slowly. "Just because Jake is not his father doesn't mean that you are. You took precautions, you...*weren't* careless. There could have been other men."

He'd thought of the possibility of other men—many times—but he didn't really believe it. Not for a minute. The Cassandra he'd known then had been shy and hesitant. It had been hard enough to believe that she'd turned to someone she knew as well as Jake. He couldn't believe there'd been others. And besides, he *knew* that no matter how many men there'd been, the child was his.

Gray shook his head, ruthlessly casting aside her arguments. "Careful doesn't offer any guarantees, Cass. Not then, not now. You know that. And *I* know that you and I share a child. Did you think I came here unprepared? That I wouldn't do my homework? I've been to the library, located all the school news in the local papers. I've seen his photos, Cassie."

"Then you know he looks like me." She stepped to the side, out of his reach, an air of triumph in her eyes.

"He looks like you," Gray admitted. "Except, Cassie, for that...something in his eyes. Other people might not see it, but I look in the mirror every day and I recognize that look, Cass. In him. In me. It's just a touch of something, but it's there. Definitely there."

She began to shake her head, but she didn't mouth the words this time.

"Admit it, Cassandra. Long ago and far away, you and I once made a baby."

Cassie's eyes were bleak, wary, frightened, when she finally looked up. "Maybe that's true, but he's mine now," she whispered. "Rob's a happy, carefree little boy. He's so very young. He's not built to be one of the lofty, rule-the-world Alexanders, and I won't risk having him hurt by trying to make him fit in your world. Not ever. He's not an Alexander," she insisted.

In the distance, down the long dirt road, came a smudge of blue and the creaking sound of a van that needed new shocks. Cassie closed her eyes. She wrapped her arms around herself and rocked slightly, and Gray knew without a doubt that his son was in that vehicle.

"Gray. Please go," she pleaded. He'd never heard a Pratt beg. He'd never seen Cassie look so wounded.

Okay, he'd taken the first step, shoved her back against the wall, but she was probably right. A man didn't just show up and expect a ten-year-old boy to welcome a stranger as a father, no matter the situation. He'd give her time to talk to her child.

"All right," he conceded. "I'll go—for now. But understand that I'll be back, Cassie. Now that I know, I won't let it alone. He's my son, too, and I won't allow any more time to pass before I claim him."

She looked up at him, her arms still tightly clutching herself as he climbed in his car.

"Two days," he said simply. "I'll give you two days to tell him, and then I'll expect to meet my son come hell or high water. Don't think I'll let it drop, Cass."

Gray passed the van on the road, a blur of children's hands and faces pressed against the windows. And then it was gone before he had time to search for his son in the crowd. But he remembered the pictures he'd seen, and the woman who had once made him forget all reason.

That wouldn't happen now. He was a man with his head

on straight, and he knew he and Cassie Pratt had once made a serious mistake, an unforgivable mistake, one they wouldn't make again. But he also knew exactly where his duty lay, and he had always believed in duty above all. He would be a father to his son, with or without Cassandra Pratt's cooperation.

Cassie watched Gray's car pass the van. The man she'd once worshiped, leaving; the boy her very heart beat for, coming home at the end of the day.

"What am I going to do?" she whispered to the silence.

Gray should have been just a memory. Instead he had been here, on her land, a very real man, with whiskey-brown eyes that burned and accused, with shoulders broad enough to shut out the sun. He had touched her and...

Dear God. Cassie shuddered. She braced her back against the front door, leaning against it as if she could shut out unwelcome sensations. She could. *She would.* But she couldn't beat back her panic, because...because...

Gray knows about Rob. He knows. The thought made her breath catch high in her chest. *He knows and he's determined to take over his parental responsibilities.*

"No. No, please, no."

Her son was so much more than a responsibility. What's more, Gray Alexander and the child tooling down the road had absolutely nothing in common outside of DNA. The Alexander men had their futures laid out for them long before they were born. They followed the path of success with steely determination, while Robbie had a custard-soft heart and all the ambition of a newborn puppy. Bringing Gray together with Rob would only create a world of disappointment and pain for her son.

Watching the van pull up in front of her house, Cassie made a promise to herself. She wasn't going to let anyone snatch Rob away from her and transplant him onto rocky, infertile Alexander soil.

She wasn't ever again going to let herself dream of Gray in her bed, naked and greedy and reaching for her. The thought leaped from nowhere and froze her on the spot.

Damn the man. The sensation of his fingers beneath her chin still lingered. She closed her eyes, pressed her own palm to her skin as if to rub away Gray's touch...or to savor it.

No, she couldn't go there, didn't want to. But she wondered how many other women had felt the same way. Many, she was sure, and it shouldn't matter to her. It didn't.

The door of the van opened and her child tumbled out, all arms and legs and smiles. "Mom!"

She smiled back, forcing Gray to the depths of her mind. "Welcome home, tiger. Bailey and I missed you."

"Mom, Mom, I've gotta tell you—"

"Thanks for everything, Faye," she said to the driver. Cassie tilted her head, crossed her arms sternly. "Rob," she admonished.

He stopped dead in his tracks, his eyes wide and confused for a second. Then he shrugged sheepishly as he turned. "Oh yeah, Mrs. Phillips. Thanks for the ride and for letting us stay overnight."

"Glad to have you, Rob." The mother in the van grinned and waved as she took off down the road.

As soon as the van was out of sight, Cassie gave her son a hug. "Now, what was it that you wanted to tell me?"

Rob's eyes lit up. "Joey's got a litter of kittens, and there's this one that's so small, Mom. He's not gonna make it if someone doesn't take care of him. I know I could—"

"Rob." Cassie's voice was stern. "Not another."

Her son's ten-year-old smile faded and his eyes turned anxious. He hunched his still-skinny shoulders. "I'll make room, Mom. I promise."

Cassie sighed, ruffling his dark hair. "I know you will,

Rob.'' She also knew her child would worry himself sick if that kitten died and he hadn't tried to save it.

He looked up with ''please'' in his eyes, worry lines marring his young forehead.

Blowing out a breath, Cassie nodded. ''All right, you *did* set the bird free last week.''

And it had been hard for him to release the sparrow whose wing had mended, but he had done it. Not that it mattered. Next spring there would probably be another wounded bird. And maybe a lizard, a lost puppy or an orphaned bunny.

''Thanks, Mom,'' he said with a whoosh of relief. ''You got anything to eat? I'm starving.''

Clearly things were back to normal now that the issue of the kitten had been settled. Rob was always starving. He was such...a kid.

Overcome with sudden love for the child who had changed her life and turned it right-side-up at last, Cassie slung an arm around his shoulder, turning him toward the house.

''You okay, Mom?''

''Sure, just getting you some food.''

''You hugged me twice.''

She had, and she didn't usually, not since he'd moved into his please-don't-embarrass-me phase. But today had been different.

Today, Gray had come and threatened her world. He'd made her shake and remember and fear.

But Rob didn't know that. And she wasn't going to tell him. For years he'd simply known his father hadn't been able to be around when he was born. He wondered sometimes, though, she was sure. She'd never told Rob he hadn't been wanted by his father, of course, but she'd known all too well that Gray's life had been built on a grand scheme for success and an unexpected child had never been a part of that plan. And she'd known way too much about forced fatherhood, about men who made their children feel like impediments to their own dreams. She hadn't wanted her son to become a duty, not when he'd been new and small and frail, and especially not now that he was an eager little colt who could be easily damaged.

Gray had wanted children—when the time was right, and apparently the time was right now, for Gray. He was ready to claim his son. She just wasn't ready to let him do that.

Realizing that Rob was looking at her, still wondering at her unusual behavior, she smiled down at him. "Hey, isn't a mother entitled to two hugs now and then? On special days?"

He eyed her suspiciously. "Today's a special day?"

She crossed her arms, tilted her head. "Well, it *is* the first day you've come home without a rip in your shirt in the last week. That ranks with me."

"Mo-om."

"'Mo-om,'" she repeated with a grin. "Hey, I'm not teasing you. This is progress. This is really good stuff. Come on, let's go get you a big bowl of macaroni and cheese."

He nodded his agreement as they entered the house. "Hey, who was in the car that was pulling out of our drive a few minutes ago? Anyone I know?"

Cassie's hand froze on the knob. "No, no one you've met."

He nodded seriously. "Must have been a friend of yours, then."

She'd spent less than twenty-four hours in close quarters with Gray Alexander. She'd certainly never been a part of his crowd. "No, not a friend."

Rob nodded like a ten-year-old wizened man. "Then was it some kind of a politician?" His tone clearly indicated that a bank robber would have been a better prospect. "One of those guys came to Joey's while I was there, and his dad said that men like that would try to smile and talk you out of everything you have. If I'm not here, don't let anyone like that in the house, Mom. I hope you sent him on his way."

"I did, Rob," she agreed. "I sent him away."

But Gray had promised to be back. Cassie hoped it wasn't true. She hoped once the shock of learning that one of his "relationships" had resulted in a child had passed, he would change his mind about wanting to meet his son.

She hoped with all of her being, because if Gray came back, he would definitely try to talk her out of everything she had, everything in the world that held meaning for her.

And she would have to fight, to pit herself against the power the Alexanders held in their hands instead of running this time.

She would have to see Gray again and know he was not the dream lover who could turn her world golden and glowing just by smiling at her. He was the man who would steal her happiness.

Chapter Two

"I don't take in boarders, mister. There's not enough room in my house for something like that."

The old man, owner of the orchard across the road from Cassie's house, shook his head at Gray.

"And there isn't anyone else who would do that? I know there are no motels in Hightower." Gray knew because he'd driven from one end of the small town to the other in thirty seconds flat. It had been two days since he'd called on Cass and he'd spent them in a town miles away, waiting for her to call the number he'd relayed to her machine. He hadn't wanted to go home and answer questions. Especially when he didn't know many of the answers. Yet.

"Nope. No one I know of." The man continued digging at the weeds in his flower bed.

Frustration rose in Gray like a billowing cloud from an awakening volcano. She hadn't called. She wasn't going to call, and it wasn't the first time in his life that she had put him in his place this way. Only this time was different. Cassie was no longer just the girl who invaded his nighttime dreams so that he awoke, aroused and alone, his body fighting his need. No, now she was the woman standing between him and his son. And this time he wouldn't be gotten rid of so easily.

"Look," he said, bending to help the man pull a dandelion from the path of a struggling rosebush. "I have some business that absolutely requires me to stay in the area for a short time. Isn't there any way? I'd be willing to pay you quite well for the use of whatever room you have."

The man stopped fussing with the weeds. He looked up at Gray. "Don't have any room, but I've got an old travel trailer. Got a bit of space at the edge of my orchard."

Gray knew he did. He'd seen the wide strip of green that bordered Cassie's land. Instantly he pulled out his wallet. "A trailer will do just fine," he confirmed. "Thank you."

"Don't thank me yet. I haven't agreed to your proposition. What's your name, son? I like to know who I'm doing business with."

Gray told him and the man raised both brows and whistled.

"Those Alexanders?" he asked. "The ones from Misunderstood?"

"Exactly," Gray acknowledged. "Do I pass muster?"

"You give me some solid identification and a hundred fifty dollars a night and we've got a deal."

Gray raised both brows. Under other circumstances he would be arguing the man down to a reasonable price—and he would win. The man was offering him the use of a circle of ground and a trailer of unknown origins for one hundred fifty dollars a night. It was robbery, but it would get him practically into Cassie's front yard.

He pulled out some bills and forked over the cash. No argument.

A short time later he was on the phone in his car.

Three rings and then the click of the receiver being raised.

"Hello." The soft swirl of Cassie's voice washed over him. Low and husky and hesitant, it filled him with heat, made him think of the faint scent of rose petals on wind, fresh-as-cream skin, and wild, deep kisses. It reminded him way too much of a jeweled spring evening when he'd been totally lost in lust.

Stupid, he thought, clenching the receiver so tightly that the plastic turned warm, the pads of his fingers flattened against the slick surface. He'd obviously been young and way too impulsive back then, but this was now, and now was different. A pair of deep blue eyes and a please-touch-me voice couldn't make him forget why he was here or what was at stake. Not by a long shot.

"You didn't call, Cass," he said simply, pushing the past aside.

He thought he heard a gasp but he wasn't sure.

"Gray—where are you?" Her voice was suddenly strained.

"Not far enough away for you, apparently. Look, Cass, I'm coming over. Have you talked to Rob?"

She hadn't. Of course she hadn't.

The silence dragged on, but he could hear the fidget of fingers on the cord, her slight, soft breathing.

"All right, give me an hour?" she finally asked. "Just an hour. Then come and we'll talk."

"And you'll spirit my son away?"

Cassie let out a soft sigh. "He's going to a friend's house this morning, anyway. If you're going to keep showing up, then I want to do this right, to prepare him. I think you and I should compare notes before I tell him anything. You don't just drop a father on a boy from out of the blue."

Maybe she was right about that, but…

"It didn't have to be this way, Cass. You could have

given me a choice eleven years ago. I would have done the right thing and married you.''

The silence was so enormous, so complete and still that for a moment Gray thought she had hung up. ''Cass?''

''Everyone isn't meant for marriage, Gray. I'm not,'' she said simply.

And that was that. Stark. Conclusive. No argument.

''I see. You weren't completely sure of that eleven years ago. It was one of the things we talked about that day.''

They had talked about many things, her growing uncertainty about marriage had been one. His belief in purely practical unions had been another. They had, in fact, had little in common, but their bodies had apparently not known that, because he had wanted her. Intensely. The pleasure had stolen his mind and his sense of who and what and where he had been. Sweet, painful pleasure.

Gray took a deep breath. He pushed back from the wild misguided memories of Cassie naked and silken in his arms. ''You told me you didn't believe a marriage could work without some heavy-duty, once-in-a-millennium love,'' he agreed, ''but I would have thought the prospect of a baby might have changed your mind.''

''I knew I could give Rob what he needed most,'' she said simply.

''And you've done that.''

She hesitated, the tiniest of pauses. ''I think so. He's happy. We have a good life here.'' Her voice was hushed but certain.

''Cass.'' Gray couldn't keep the censure from his voice.

''Don't bother saying it. I'm sure that doesn't change things as far as you're concerned. I'm just telling you that...Rob feels things deep inside, strongly. If you're dead set on showing up, then okay, we have to talk. Come over in an hour,'' she offered again. ''And Gray?''

''Yes?''

''I did consider telling you the truth once, but it just

wouldn't have worked. Maybe it sounds trite and foolish and even cruel, but I thought I was doing what was best for everyone at the time. I still do."

The click of the phone prevented Gray from answering, but in truth it was just as well. He didn't know what he would have said, anyway. For once in his life, a smooth-talking Alexander was at a loss for words.

Pacing the floor, waiting for Gray, Cassie's heart did a spike-heeled tap dance inside her chest, sending her blood on a wild, spinning ride. Her breathing was all wrong, almost frantic, like a Lamaze lesson gone bad. And she hated reacting to Gray this way. Gray had been out of her life for years. She'd managed to eject him from her heart and mind, and once that door had closed, she'd installed a dozen locks, a few hundred dead bolts. So she knew she wasn't in any danger emotionally. She couldn't be.

"I'm fine," she said, unclenching her fingers just to prove her point.

She was absolutely certain this lurching anticipation warring with an urge to hide under the nearest box had nothing to do with the fact that she'd once glowed in Gray's arms or that he'd tasted parts of her body that had never seen the sun. No, it didn't. This was just pure, maternal fear, what any mother would feel when her child was facing possible danger.

That was all. Her concern was strictly for Rob right now, and it was a very real concern, no doubt about that. No doubt that she'd do whatever it took to protect him, either. From anything that threatened his well-being... including his father.

As the last thought formed, solidified, Cass saw Gray's car coming down the road. She clutched the window ledge to keep herself from fleeing. Life had been less complicated in many ways these last years since she'd stopped spending her days looking for the man and no way was she going to start falling into that trap again, but neither would she cower behind the house, either.

Forcing herself to take long, slow breaths, she purposefully started toward the door, then swung it aside. "Come in," she tried to call to the man exiting his car, but the words died in her throat.

The windows in Gray's car had been open, and the wind had sifted through his hair like a woman's seeking fingers. He was facing her, one lean, strong hand resting on the car. His jeans molded to muscled thighs, his white shirt was open at the throat. His lips curved upward ever so slightly as Bailey pushed past her and sat on the porch like some monster dog security guard, and the whole effect of Gray's dark, tell-me-your-secrets eyes combined with that potent Alexander smile was way too much like... seduction.

Get a grip, Pratt. Get a life. Get a brain, some sort of a link with reality, she told herself.

"Let's talk, Cass," Gray said, cutting off her wandering thoughts, eyeing her bare feet, making her feel half naked even though she'd spent half her life running around without shoes. He gestured to a basket on the passenger seat of his car. "I've got food."

Whistles and bells went off in Cass's head. For the life of her, she couldn't keep from remembering how Gray had once told her something that had sounded much the same, yet not the same at all. *I've got protection,* he'd said just before they'd twined themselves about each other and taken the life-altering step that had brought them to this moment in time.

It was silly, completely idiotic, but she couldn't look at that basket. Absolutely not.

"Cass?"

She raised her chin, slid one foot behind her other ankle. This was beyond silly. It was teenage-dream silly, and she would never be a dreamy-eyed teenager ever again.

Carefully she lifted one brow. "You brought a picnic basket? You thought I might poison your lunch? I thought the Alexanders weren't scared of anything, Gray."

Gray rubbed one hand over his clean-shaven jaw and blew out a breath.

"Maybe I just thought my sudden intrusion might have interfered with your own meal." He whisked back the car door. "Maybe I thought that if we were going to have to get along and get some things settled, we should start right now. With a peace offering," he said.

Lifting the basket from the car, he started toward her, not waiting for an invitation. "I thought feeding you might be a small place to start."

In just two easy strides he was at the edge of her porch.

It was clear he wasn't giving her a choice this time. He intended to invade her home. But, of course, self-assurance was bred in his bones. She remembered how good that self-assurance had always looked to her, and darn it, it still looked good. But now that smooth confidence he'd been born with was going to cause her nothing but trouble. Gray wasn't the type to back down, and he looked like he was planning to enter her house even if he had to pick her up and place her somewhere else to do it.

She dragged in air, stood straighter, fussed with the end of her braid. Silly, she reminded herself again. The man was just being civil. And civility was probably a wise move right now, Cassie conceded. The only rational option open, after all. When two people were being polite, they didn't feel...other more physical sensations.

She nodded tightly, ignoring her off-limits thoughts.

"Come on in." Stepping aside, she motioned him into her home. "And thank you. For bringing lunch."

Reaching for the door, Cass felt Gray's heat at her back as he fell into step behind her. His fingers closed over her own when she grasped the doorknob.

"Let me," he said gruffly.

The warmth of his large hand over her own smaller one startled Cass. She felt the contact shimmy through her entire body, and quickly pulled away, letting him have his way.

"Mmm, all right, thank you," she agreed, trying to sound nonchalant, to pretend his touch had been nothing. It *had* been nothing for him, she was sure, a mere formality. He was an Alexander, after all, and even Hugh Alexander had been frigidly formal with her, right up until the moment when he threatened to make her parents suffer for her own presumptuousness. The memory was like a splinter, there before you knew it, painful once you'd realized it was too late for prevention.

She inhaled as deeply as she dared without giving him a visible clue to her nervousness and moved into the house. Her parents were gone now, but Rob was very real. She had to be careful, to cross this field of land mines one tiny step at a time. She would treat Gray the way she treated her customers. With distant courtesy. Maybe he only wanted to see his son once. Maybe after his curiosity was satisfied, he would go, and she could forget about the Alexanders forever. She cleared her throat, turned to Gray.

"I'm sorry if I was rude on the phone. I didn't even bother asking you if this time would be convenient. Perhaps you need to get back to your business?" There. That was more like her usual composure.

"That's not an issue. I've got all the time we need, Cass." Gray's voice was a slow drawl, a stroke of sound.

Cassie managed to keep from gasping. *So much for composure,* she mused silently. "I don't think we'll need much time."

Gray looked at the tense line of Cassie's body. She was wishing him gone again, and the thought chafed, burned. This was not going to be easy. She'd become a fighter in the past few years. That much was evident.

And when he looked around her house, something else

became evident. She'd created a home all her own, for while the outside of the small square house was almost cabinlike, the inside was anything but stark. Bowls of red and white blossoms laced with baby's breath graced modest tables and scented the air. Small woven rugs were scattered about the golden floor, and lace curtains let sparkling patterns of sunlight into the small room. There was a stack of wildlife magazines in an old basket by an aging rocking chair, and a shelf filled with well-worn books. The furniture was ragged in places, but invitingly overstuffed. This was a home, not just a house.

But he had barely managed to register that fact when Cassie slid off into the kitchen. He followed her, watched as she set out napkins and food, as she nervously let the knives and forks clank against each other.

"Gray, about Rob—" she began.

"Yes. Rob. What does our son know about...us?" he asked.

Her hands froze on a red ironstone plate. She looked up at Gray with eyes that were undeniably beautiful, but more than that...worried. Sad. Damn near scared to death. He had an unexplainable urge to tell her he would make everything all right, one he quickly squelched. After all, this woman owed him, had taken his son from him without even letting him know he had a son. Besides, both of them knew this situation was sticky. It was already way too late for an easy fix.

"I didn't tell him much. He simply knows that his father couldn't be with us, that we couldn't marry." She barely breathed the words.

Gray moved to stand opposite her. He planted both hands on the wood of the table. "Then you lied to him. I told you, we *could* have married."

Standing straighter, Cassie thrust her chin high. "No, I didn't lie. You and I could never have been a pair. I don't want marriage, and even if I did...we're too different."

"It doesn't take people who are the same to make a marriage."

Her eyes were clear and blue and filled with conviction when she stared back at him.

"When the differences are as great as ours are, it does. You don't even believe love has to be an ingredient of a marriage."

No, he didn't. His uncle had almost stopped living when his aunt had left home. His own father had become a shell of his former self when his mother had divorced him. He himself had foolishly been half in love with Cass when she had turned her back on him. So, no, he didn't believe in love even though he believed in marriage. More than that, he didn't *want* love, would sidestep it if it ever came his way again.

Just as Cassie wanted to sidestep him. Gray blew out a breath. It was obvious from her comments just the other day what she thought of his family and all that they stood for.

Gray looked around at her simple house so different from his own, and he knew that she was right about one thing. They lived in worlds that were completely different Their goals and beliefs were nothing alike. If they had married, theirs would have been one of the ones that wouldn't have worked.

"I could have still been here for him. And for you," he argued. "And I'm here now, Cass. I'm not leaving."

She placed her hands on the table, leaning closer. "My son and I are not your responsibility, Gray. One quick act of procreation is not a binding contract."

He studied her lips as she spoke, that soft, silky voice. "It wasn't quick," he argued.

Hot rose crept up from the neckline of her blouse.

"And it wasn't binding," she added.

"It was to me. And how do you think I feel knowing that my son thinks I abandoned him for some vague reason? I *could* have been with him, Cass. You know that I would have."

"I'll tell him it was my fault."

"You do that," he agreed. "But it won't change a thing. I don't walk away from my messes."

Cassie sucked in a deep breath. She glared at him and her hands curled into fists. "Rob isn't a mess."

Gray reached out. He took her hand in his, stroked his thumb against her own. "No, he's not. He's my son. My flesh and blood, the same as he is yours," he said, holding her warmth against his, trying to make her see that he was, indeed, human. "And I want to be a father to him, but you're the key, Cass. You can make it easy or hard for us. Don't you want him to have a father? I'll do my best to be a good one."

She closed her eyes as if she didn't want to hear his words, as if shutting out the sight of him would make him go away. Her hand trembled in his. A shudder ripped through her, and when she opened her eyes they were bright with unshed tears.

"I don't want him to just be someone's duty," she said, biting her lip.

"I'd never make him feel that way."

Cassie looked at the man who was asking for her help, the man who had come immediately once he had learned he had a son. She knew his deep sense of duty was what had brought him here. But she also believed in the truth of his words. Gray had a way of making a person feel special, no matter what the true motivations were for his actions. He'd made her feel very special once even when she'd known all along that she had simply been in a convenient place at a convenient time. It was only afterward that she had faced the truth. And so she knew that if her son was a simple responsibility to Gray, then Rob would probably never know. Only she would. She also knew one thing more: she couldn't hide the truth from her son any longer. If Gray knew the truth, other people would in time. Now that everyone knew Jake was not Rob's father, people would want to know who was. And with Gray breaking off his engagement and spending his hours in Hightower, the secret would be no secret any longer.

The piper had returned, and he wanted cash up front.

She took a deep breath as she faced the truth and the deeper, scarier secret that had finally surfaced, the one she'd thought would never come to light.

"What will he think, what in the world will he think, Gray, when I tell him you were only seventy-five miles away all the time?"

Gray reached out. He slid his thumb over the worry lines that had formed on her forehead.

"I don't know, Cass, but it looks like we're going to have a lot of explaining to do. Nothing quick and easy, either."

"I don't want him scared," she whispered, "or thinking we're going to turn into the Brady Bunch just because his father is here now."

"I don't want him scared, either," he said. "I— Damn, I don't want to, but I suppose I could try to give him a little time to get to know me before we spring the whole truth on him."

Cassie studied his face to see if he really meant what he said, or if he was just trying to see how eager she would be to latch on to that possibility. Gray's reluctant smile made his brown eyes even warmer than they normally were. She suspected that given the truth, Gray would have stepped forward to claim his role as father long ago, because it was what he'd felt he should do. But she hadn't expected him to be so fervent in his pursuit of his duty.

"Do you think that would make it easier for him?" she asked carefully.

"I don't know," he said. "I've never been a father, but I want the chance to be one, and I'm afraid that if we hit

Rob too hard, he'll run before he and I even have a chance to become acquainted. And I wouldn't blame him for his anger.''

Cassie winced. She *had* had good reasons for hiding her son's existence, and once she'd known she was pregnant, there'd been no way she could have stayed in Misunderstood where the Alexanders and their pride permeated the town. Running had seemed the only way. Letting people think that she had been abandoned by the true father had seemed...safe.

But that time was gone. Her son was going to meet the past now and she wanted him eased into it as painlessly as possible.

As she sat down across the table from the man who would now be a part of her life whether she liked it or not, Cass nodded.

''Thank you—for that, for the extra time. We'll let him get to know you. I'll tell him the truth, that we were once acquainted. You can come here now and then, maybe on weekends, to see him. As a friend.''

And maybe that would be enough for Gray, she hoped. Maybe Hugh Alexander would never even discover that he had an illegitimate grandchild, descended from the Pratts that had disgusted him so.

Gray was shaking his head. ''Not just weekends. I've lost too many years, Cass. I'm not going to waste any more time.'' He took a bite of the sandwich she had handed to him.

''What does that mean?'' She stared at her own sandwich, picked it up, wondering if there was any way she could possibly swallow anything right now.

''It means I intend to be close. I've rented a plot of land across the road from you, and a trailer.''

Cassie blinked hard. She dropped her sandwich. ''You've done what? You'll be where? All the time?''

Gray studied the sudden stubborn line of her lips.

"You've got some objections? Changed your mind? Are we going to have to do this the hard way, Cass?"

Leaning into his space, Cassie stared straight into his eyes. "Yes, I have some objections about this whole thing. Wouldn't you if you were me? And I'm not ducking out on the blame, either. If you say you wanted to know about Rob when he was born, then I suppose there's just no way I should have kept him from you. But this... I mean, an Alexander in a trailer? Just how are you going to explain that one, Gray? What will you say you're doing? And how can you take time away from the Alexander empire, the businesses, the land? I thought you had a mayoral campaign to run."

He grinned at her consternation, the first time he'd let loose with a full-fledged smile since he'd parked that car in her drive two days ago, and her heart flipped around like a bit of dry paper carried helplessly on the wind.

"When I learned about you and Rob, everything changed, Cass. Running for any kind of office is in the past now that I have a child to think of. And since I ended my engagement, people will probably just assume I've gone off to nurse a broken heart. My father will take over for me temporarily. There's time to get to know my son and indulge myself with a camping vacation near the home of an old acquaintance."

With his last words, Cassie remembered what little she'd known of Gray, what her time with him had been like. A day of sun and passion and feverish touches.

Gray practically in her house, all the time, day and night was...not to be endured without squirming.

"Couldn't you find a better place to stay?" she asked.

"Are you offering?"

She blinked, sucked in air. "I don't think that would be wise."

"No," he agreed. "It wouldn't be, especially since

we've agreed we don't have what it takes to make a future. It wouldn't do to live together in close quarters.''

Cass pressed a hand to her chest. She breathed deeply. ''I didn't mean we couldn't be adults, but...''

''I wasn't worried that we couldn't be adults, Cass. On the contrary, closed up in this small space, I'm more than aware that we're both adults. The trailer will do me fine until we decide to tell Rob the truth. By then, I'm hoping that you'll let him stay with me now and then.''

Gray's casual and matter-of-fact reference to the something silently sizzling between them caught Cass off guard. The thought of letting Rob stay with him sometime in the near future made her flinch. Things were going too fast.

''I'm sorry. I need to get back to work. I asked a neighbor's son to watch the store, but I can't leave him there for long,'' she said suddenly, starting to rise to her feet.

Gray quickly moved to pull out her chair.

''I can manage,'' she said, pushing back.

But when her napkin fluttered to the floor, he retrieved it, handing it to her as though it were a rose.

He was close, way too close, and her mind was not functioning—or maybe it was functioning in all the wrong ways.

She took the napkin reluctantly, trying not to brush his fingers against her own.

''I'm sorry. I guess I'm just not used to that kind of chivalry,'' she said to hide her awkwardness and lack of grace. ''The world doesn't work that way anymore.''

''My world does,'' he said. ''And it's not a question of a woman's being able. If you're a mother, you're capable of handling a whole lot more than a chair and a napkin, but...''

''But you're an Alexander, and you were taught your manners while you were still in the womb,'' she said lightly. ''I know, Gray. You were always polite.''

''Not always,'' he corrected, a gruff note in his voice.

And she remembered that no, he hadn't always been polite. He had been demanding, fevered and impatient.

She had been just as impatient.

But that had been one day in time, one day that should never have happened, except...they had made a beautiful son that day.

And now they would share that son.

She didn't know how she would manage to be with Grayson Alexander every day and keep him from seeing that he still called forth impatient urges in her.

But she would. She had to.

Cassie tried to remember that as she saw Gray to the door and back to his car. She tried to look upon him the way they were going to present him to Rob, as an "acquaintance."

It wasn't working.

"I'll be back tonight," he said.

She took a deep breath and managed to nod even though panic was already beginning to climb through her body.

Cassie couldn't help looking across the road to the place where she assumed Gray would be setting up shop.

"You'll have time to talk to him," he promised, as if he were reading her mind. "I'll spend today taking care of business. There are a few things I need to remind my father to do."

His father. He'd mentioned him once before. Cassie looked at him, felt her panic increasing. The threat Hugh Alexander represented ballooned in her mind. Had she really thought she could keep this simple? Was there any chance she could even begin to shield her child from all the troubles and threats the truth was going to unleash?

"What will your family think of all this?" She barely managed to choke out the words.

But she knew already. She knew what they would think.

Hugh Alexander had told her years ago just what he

thought of her when he hadn't even known for sure that she'd slept with his son.

Cassie raised her chin high.

Gray was staring at her, concern in his eyes.

"No one is going to make him feel self-conscious or small, Cass," Gray assured her. "I wouldn't let that happen."

No, she was sure he would try to keep that from happening.

But maybe he wouldn't be able to stop it. And maybe it was just her the Alexanders would disapprove of. Maybe they'd try to take Rob away and turn him into one of them.

"I don't like any of this, Gray." She couldn't hold the words back. The emotion ran too deep.

"Then don't like it, Cass. But don't try to stop it, either. You can't. I wouldn't let you. It's too late to go back to yesterday."

That was the undeniable truth, Cassie thought as she watched him stride to his car, all lean muscle and broad shoulders. Because yesterday she had been a young girl spinning fairy tales about a prince who would find her and love her the way all people loved in unrealistic stories.

But this was no fairy tale staring her in the face. Gray wasn't the type to believe in love. He never had been.

Still, tonight he would be here. Crowding her. Pushing her. The tornado had been unleashed and, wish as she might, she couldn't keep the wild winds at bay. All she could do was love her child and hope Gray Alexander wouldn't blow her world apart completely.

Chapter Three

Rob had been home for twenty minutes and Cassie still hadn't approached him about Gray. The hands on the clock were spinning way too fast. In no time at all, Gray would be done with his tasks. He'd be back here getting that darned trailer into place. And she had better stop messing around and start preparing Rob for what was to come.

Putting out the sign that told her customers she could be found at the house, Cassie reluctantly wandered out the back door.

"Rob?" she called softly, not wanting to startle him. When he was with his animals, as he was so much on these summer days, he was in a different world. Having spent her own childhood being startled from sleep or whatever daydream she was in by the frightening, too loud sounds of anger, she was always cautious about bringing her own child back to the real world softly, slowly.

He turned as she neared him and gave her a smile.

"Hi, Mom. You need something?"

Cassie willed the muscles of her face to relax. "Just

your attention and help for a few minutes. Would you believe I've actually invited company for dinner?''

Rob's eyes rounded. He stopped stroking the fur of the cat he had been tending. ''You mean like grown-up company? Coming to our house to eat? Who is it?''

She shrugged, struggling to keep her voice from wobbling, her hands from trembling with nervousness. ''An old acquaintance. Remember that car that was here the other day? Well, I don't really know Grayson too well, but we *did* once go to the same school. He came by today and told me he'd be doing some camping. He's talked Mr. Moser into renting him a bit of land and a trailer. I thought maybe you'd like to meet him. He could get a chance to see what a great kid I've got.''

Rob narrowed his eyes and looked at her. ''He's camping in a cherry orchard? Our Mr. Moser's cherry orchard? Why?''

She managed to hold her shaking smile. ''Well, he's just—camping.''

Her son still didn't look convinced. ''Maybe he wants to date you.''

''Rob.'' Cassie's voice broke. ''He's not looking for a date. Believe me.''

''And he's an old friend?''

Her son had crossed his arms, like a father interrogating his teenage daughter about the guy taking her to the prom.

''An acquaintance,'' she insisted, pulling him into the kitchen. ''From when I lived in Misunderstood. Come on, give me a hand. We're going to cook tonight.'' An outdoor meal, she'd decided. Neutral territory. Safe territory.

To her surprise, he followed her without protest, dragging out the pans she asked for, hustling for the ingredients she requested. He was quiet for a long time. Then he looked up from the carrot he was trying to peel.

''Did this guy know my father?''

Cassie froze. She stopped reaching for the refrigerator handle. She turned to her son.

"Yes," she said quietly. "He did."

Long minutes passed. Silent minutes.

"Do you ever miss having a father?" she couldn't help asking.

Of course they had discussed his father's absence before. It was a topic that did come up now and then, but today was different. Today someone from her past was here, and that was the reason Rob had thought of the man who had fathered him.

"Rob?" she asked gently when he still hadn't answered.

He looked at her, his blue eyes serious as he bit down on his lip. "Sure. Sometimes. But not too much," he added hastily.

Dark, gritty guilt settled over her. "Are you trying to keep from hurting my feelings?"

He raised one shoulder, continued at his task. "I wouldn't give you up just to have a dad, Mom."

She nodded, pretending to busy herself, turning her back to him as emotion washed through her. He loved her just as she loved him. A lot. A whole heck of a lot, but...he *did* want to be like other boys. He *did* want a father. How would he feel when he finally found out he could have had one? What would she say to him then?

"You sure this guy isn't looking for a date?" he asked suddenly.

"I'm sure," she said, dredging up a smile. "You don't have to get all huffy and parental. I'm positive he's not interested in me."

No, Gray had never been interested in her. Not really.

He'd simply been acting like any young, hot-blooded male that long ago day. He'd taken what was offered. And now he'd come to claim what hadn't been offered. He wanted the son he felt she'd stolen from him.

* * *

"Nice dog you've got there." Gray held his hand out to Bailey, but he kept his gaze on his son who simply nodded his agreement. Cass had been right. Rob looked even more like her in person than he did in his pictures, all dark hair and blue eyes. And she—she was clearly nervous, snapping out the legs on a folding table, shooing him away when he tried to help.

"I can do this alone, Gray," she assured him.

Of course she could. She'd been doing everything alone for eleven years. Thinking back to the way she'd dressed at seventeen, in clothing that never quite seemed to fit, Gray suspected she'd been doing things for herself for a long time before that. And she'd had a baby all by herself, too. She hadn't even thought to ask for his assistance.

Should she have? He'd met her one day, been swept away by the spell she'd cast on him, and had taken her virginity as if he deflowered virgins twice a day and three times on Sundays instead of once in a lifetime. Was it a surprise she hadn't expected him to be interested in his child?

She'd been strong, and yes, alone. That fact shamed him, stung, and it made him angry. Gray wasn't sure who he was more angry at, Cass or himself, and so he turned to the only true innocent. He stared into the too suspicious eyes of his child.

"I hear you have a way with animals," he said. "How many do you have right now?"

Rob sucked in his lip as if he didn't want to talk. At a look from his mother, he caved and let out a sigh. "One dog, a cat with five kittens, two toads, a rabbit, a hamster and a box turtle. Mom drew the line at field mice."

Cassie smiled and handed Gray a stack of plates. "Hey, no complaints. I didn't even squeal when you brought home Tim Daley's pet tarantula when he went on vacation."

"Brave lady," Gray said, and he wasn't just talking

about animals. No matter how angry he was with Cass, he couldn't discount her bravery…or her stubbornness. He'd just bet that Rob had argued for the field mice passionately and still lost. The thought made him smile. "Do all your pets have names?" he asked his child.

Rob looked at him as if he'd just asked something stupid, which, Gray figured, he probably had.

"Do you think you'll be staying here long?" the boy asked instead, eyeing the slightly lopsided, somewhat rusty trailer.

So it was going to be like that, was it? Difficult.

"Rob," his mother admonished.

"Sorry." But no way did the kid sound sorry. Gray wasn't sure he could blame him. Having a strange man set up camp within spitting distance of your house had to be a bit suspect. Gray wondered if he might not have been smarter to stay in the hotel he'd slept in the night before and make the long drive back every day. But something told him that would be even more unacceptable. What reason could he give for coming by every day? At least this way, Rob viewed him as simply some strange city guy out to try his hand at the outdoor life.

"I'm not sure. That'll depend on a number of things," he admitted. "But I'd like to spend some time recharging my batteries. I thought you and your mother might have some suggestions about some good ways to spend my time around here."

Rob frowned as if he was thinking…of some good way to get rid of him, Gray figured.

Cassie fidgeted with the food. "There's…some pretty decent fishing around here, isn't there, Rob?" Okay, she didn't sound wildly enthusiastic herself, but at least she was being polite. Gray gave her points for trying.

Not Rob, apparently. He was staring at his mother as if she'd mutated into a stranger in the past few minutes. Still, he responded to the look she was giving him. "Yeah, there's fishing, but I don't know the best spots. Jake takes me when he comes. He's the one who knows where to catch the big ones."

"Jake Walker?" Gray already knew the answer to that question just as he knew that Jake came here to visit when he could. And there was a sting to realizing Jake Walker had shown his son all the things *he* should have been showing him.

What's more, Jake had slept in Cassie's house. She trusted the man in a way she would have never trusted *him.*

Gray brushed back his instant irritation. Rob was smiling now, talking.

"Once, Jake caught this really big trout," he was saying, holding his arms open so wide that Gray had to force himself not to raise his brows. "It was so cool watching him reel her in. Jake's some fisherman."

"I've heard he's quite a guy," Gray agreed quietly.

"You know him?" A thin trace of interest rose in Rob's voice.

"Saw him just a few days ago," Gray confirmed. Of course there was no point in telling Rob he and Jake had been eyeing each other over a bargaining table when the preservation committee was trying to decide whether or not to grant Jake's request for approval to restore his house. Or that Jake had been a witness to his own shock at discovering he had once fathered a son.

"Mom, you didn't tell me he knew Jake." It was clear from the awe in his voice that Rob considered Jake a god and Gray a mere man rendered somewhat palatable only by his connection to a deity. It was also clear from the look in Cassie's eyes that she was worried. She was genuinely scared. Because she *hadn't* told Rob he knew Jake. She hadn't told him a great many things he would probably not be pleased to know.

The world thought Jake was Rob's father. Did Rob think

the same? Did Cass wish it was so? She and Jake, after all, had similar backgrounds. She had a lot more in common with Jake Walker than she did with Gray Alexander.

He studied her as she and her son spoke softly while Cassie set out the meal and the candles that provided the only light other than the moon and stars.

She was a lady of mystery, one he had never known at all, Gray conceded. One who didn't want to know him at all, either. And one who still stirred him to instant and unwelcome desire, he forced himself to admit, watching the way her white cotton blouse kissed the peaks of her breasts when she twisted in her seat to hand him his plate.

Frustration simmered in Gray. The fact that he found her attractive was something he needed to ignore. Badly. It was what had gotten him into this situation in the first place. The memory of that past attraction was surely what was making her so jumpy, too. That and the fact that she was afraid he was going to snatch up her son and carry him away.

Hell. He had a right to be here, he told himself, turning his attention to the meal and Cass's forced attempts at conversation. Years of ground to cover, no matter what Cass wanted or didn't want. Of course he did.

But the last crumb was barely eaten when Rob looked up and pushed back from his place at the table.

"It's late, Mom. I need to check on my animals."

Gray heard the pleading in his son's voice, and for a second his thoughts faltered. No doubt about it, he was going to turn his child's world upside down, cause Cass to lie awake and wish him gone at night. But—leaving them alone now just wasn't a possibility. He had to at least let his son know his absence hadn't meant he hadn't cared.

Cassie was looking at him, a question in her eyes. Permission to leave?

"Thank you for dinner, Cassie," he said, rising as she did so. "Tomorrow I hope you'll be my guests."

Rob was looking slightly...unsure.

"Would you mind sharing your time and your mom's time with me again?" Gray asked. "You could...show me your animals. Maybe we could even go visit Jake sometime since he's pretty busy working on his house right now."

Rob's uncertain look morphed into a hint of a smile. "Really? I'd...I'd like to see Jake. He's the best."

"Someone else told me that just a few days ago. Must be true. Nice meeting you, Rob." Gray held out his hand for a man-to-man shake. Rob hesitated, then quietly stepped forward. His son had a firm grasp, Gray noted with pride. Even if he wasn't too thrilled about the man whose hand he was shaking.

Looking from his mother to Gray, Rob rocked on his heels.

"I'll help your mother clean up," Gray offered. "If that's all right with you?"

Cassie was trying to smile at her son, but her body looked tense, snap-in-the-wind brittle.

"I'll be there in just a few minutes, Rob. Don't worry, and thanks for helping out tonight."

He nodded and moved toward the house, pausing only once to look back over his shoulder before he went inside.

Gray began to gather the dishes. He felt a slim, cold hand on his arm. Cass's eyes were way too wide, full of worry.

"Not Misunderstood, Gray. I don't want him to go there."

They stood staring, perfectly still except for the breeze lifting soft tendrils of her hair.

She'd been unhappy in that town, she'd been shamed in that town, she'd run from that town.

"Okay, not Misunderstood. Not yet, anyway. I'll work out an alternate suggestion. For now."

She opened her mouth to speak. He brushed his fingers

across her lips to stop her. ''It's my home,'' he explained simply. ''But...not yet, and not without consulting you first.''

Cassie dragged in a long, deep shudder of air, but she didn't speak. Instead she turned, looked to where a light had just clicked on inside the house and Rob was moving past a window.

''He's so tall,'' Gray said, as Rob stepped beyond the window, disappearing from view again.

He looked down to the slender woman who was still facing him. She looked slightly less blown-glass-fragile now, but she still wasn't smiling. ''Yes, he's going to be a skyscraper someday,'' she said softly, her voice laced with affection for her son. ''But then, what would you expect with a mother who's five-eight and a father who's...''

''Six-two.''

''Exactly,'' she agreed. ''He's always been on the tall side, even when he was very young.''

He didn't answer, couldn't bring himself to answer, and she bit down on her lip. ''I—I'm sorry, Gray.'' She dragged the words out slowly. ''I know it doesn't mean much now, but I am sorry you didn't get to see what he was like during those years. If I had missed that...''

''I'll see him now,'' he said, trying to control the evidence of his regret.

''I do have pictures I can show you. I know it's not the same, but—''

''It'll have to be enough,'' he agreed. Gray walked around the table, moved a step closer. ''And, Cass?''

She looked up into his eyes and he found himself wanting to move even closer, to see her better in the starlight's glow now that the candles were dying.

''Dammit, Cass, I'm not going to lie. I could curse your sweet silent lips to hell and back for keeping him from me all these years, but don't—'' He let loose of a big sigh.

"Hell, don't let me make you feel too guilty. The fact is that I'd like to think I would have done things differently if I'd been in your situation, but—I don't really know that. Not for sure. What I do know is that you and I had discussed our life's goals. We'd taken precautions not to make a baby. I'd made it clear I didn't plan to marry and start a family for a number of years. I wish you'd told me. I wish I could turn back time and make you tell me, but..."

He was close enough to touch her easily now, and she looked away, as if she wished he would move back a step.

Her nervousness scraped at him. Once, he'd held her in his arms and plundered her mouth with his own. Once, she had returned his kisses with fervor and mindless need. She'd pressed herself close to him.

Gray breathed in slowly, deeply, fighting the urge to touch her and see what would happen this time. And when he felt the lightweight table move as she breathed in too deeply and bumped against it suddenly, when she flattened her palms against the tabletop as if to keep them from shaking, he *did* step away from her.

He closed his eyes at the thought that he could forget himself so easily. Bad mistake to do that when neither of them wanted this thing to progress down the wrong road again. This time he would think. He wouldn't get reckless and take a risk again. Especially when Cass wasn't about to let him make things right in the most logical way possible.

"You should get some sleep. You're probably tired," Cass said in a near-whisper and he opened his eyes to see if she was just trying to get rid of him again, but what he saw was...concern. "When you're not used to this total darkness broken only by starlight the way we are, it affects your biorhythm at first," she explained. "Even a town the size of Misunderstood had streetlights and a bit of glow when I was there."

She started to gather the remaining dishes.

"I'm fine," he assured her, "but it *has* been a long time since I even took the time to stand outside looking at the stars. It's beautiful here." And he reached for her hand even though he knew this was something he would regret later. "You have a lovely home, Cass. A wonderful son. You should be proud of all you've done here."

Shrugging one shoulder, lifting one corner of her lips slightly, she looked straight into his eyes. "I am," she said simply. "I really am," she repeated as if the thought surprised her, as if she'd never admitted such a thing.

Ignoring common sense, ignoring everything sane, he reached out and cupped her cheek with one hand.

"I came here planning to make things right, with a ring and a marriage license," he admitted.

She lifted her chin. Her jaw grew rigid beneath his fingers.

"I told you—"

"Shh," he said, trying to soothe away the effects of his autocratic suggestion. "That's what I thought at first, but I can see you're not going to buy into that idea. Now I'm just planning to invade your world for a while, to win Rob's trust, to have him come stay with me now and then, when he wants to."

She stared up at him bleakly.

"None of this is what you really want, is it?" he asked.

Shaking her head, hard, studying the concern and determination in Gray's eyes, Cassie agreed. She was feeling cornered and all she wanted to do was crawl back into her world where she had pretended he no longer existed, where he didn't assault her senses and make her realize that she had actions she had to answer for.

"I guess it's too late for what I want," she conceded. "The box has been opened and the truth has to tumble out."

"I'll play fair," he promised.

"Don't you think I know that? You always play fair. You always do the right thing."

He lived by his honor and his sense of responsibility. She followed her feelings, her fears and desires. And right now her feelings were telling her Gray was much too close, that if she wasn't careful, she would stumble right back into old bad habits she had kicked clear of.

If she didn't get rid of him real soon, she'd be watching out the window for him, listening for the sound of his voice, spinning dreams that had all the substance of soap bubbles.

"You can't stay there in this leaky trailer forever," she reasoned. "What will Rob think?"

"That I'd better pray for sunny skies?" Gray grinned. "That your old acquaintances are a bit short on common sense?"

"Gray..." she admonished, the same way she'd speak to Rob when he was avoiding the subject.

He sobered instantly, let his fingers slide along the line of her jaw. "I'm hoping he'll see he means more to me than a roof over my head, and that he'll forgive both of us for making a few wrong turns. I'm hoping that when all is said and done we'll be able to make something workable out of all this."

She nodded slowly, telling herself she wasn't even noticing the feel of his fingertips sliding against her skin, and that she wasn't susceptible to his charm anymore.

"I'll call you in the morning," he whispered, his voice vibrating through his fingertips and into her body.

She swallowed, flailing against the sweet sensations that enveloped her.

"Call me? You're in a trailer, Gray," she whispered back, struggling for sanity and reason.

"Cass, even out here among the stars, technology is ever present. I have a phone in my car, and I'll call," he promised. "You treated me tonight. Tomorrow it's my turn to take care of you and Rob."

She stilled, opening her eyes wider. "Keep it simple, please, Gray. You wouldn't try to bribe your way into my son's good graces, would you?" She tried not to think about the promises he had made to Rob about taking him to see Jake in Misunderstood. He had told her he would wait on that, but—

Slowly Gray shook his head. "I wouldn't stoop so low as to bribe him, Cass. I'll be good," he promised again. But he was too close now. When she tipped her head up, she found his lips almost upon her own. In half a heartbeat, he could be kissing her. She could be kissing him back.

Cassie tried to breathe and found she couldn't. She wanted to move and knew that if she did, she would be lost.

Gray hovered over her, the warm male scent of him surrounding her. Then slowly he raised his head.

"I'll be good," he said again, his words coming out on a long, slow breath.

But it didn't matter, Cass thought as she jerked her head up in a nod, turning away from Gray as she moved toward the house.

He could be as good as he wanted. He didn't have to bribe her, had never needed to do that. She had always had a weakness for the man. The fact that he had been the one to do the right thing in pulling back from that kiss was proof of that.

She hated being weak, was just going to have to erase that particular defect from her life, because the truth was that she couldn't afford to risk the temptation of Gray Alexander again.

A marriage between her and Gray would be loveless, empty, a marriage of duty, Gray's god. It would bring misery to her and her son, and she'd run from misery for too long to let it catch her now.

She'd run from Misunderstood, too, and now the threat of that town was staring her right in the face. What would Hugh Alexander do if Gray showed up in Misunderstood with a child, especially if even for a second, that child had caused his son to contemplate marriage with a Pratt?

The thought was unthinkable, frightening. The man wouldn't care about the welfare of one young boy. He would be ruthless if he knew. But he wouldn't, she assured herself, because she was never going to marry an Alexander. And Gray had promised her time. A little time, anyway.

By tomorrow she would have her emotions stashed away, she'd think of a way out of this tangle. By then she would be ready to face Gray without fear that she was going to screw up and slip into his arms again. It was not going to happen.

Not this time.

Chapter Four

The next morning the sound of muffled footfalls on the road drifted through the emptiness of the country dawn and crept into Cassie's consciousness. Slowly she sat up in bed.

"Rob?" she called softly, wondering why her late-sleeping son was up when the black of night had barely faded away.

Rising to her knees, she flipped the corner of the curtain back and opened the window wider.

"Go back to sleep, Cass. I'm sorry I woke you." Gray's low voice carried easily in the early morning stillness. Looking toward the road, she realized he was clad only in black shorts, his chest bare and slick from his run.

She had seen that chest damp with sweat before. The one time she had made love to Gray she had clung to those same broad shoulders as he had lowered her gently to the soft grass, kissed her, driven her crazy with the ache to have him inside her, joined to her completely.

Her fingers locked on the curtain. Her breath caught and

held, so that she had to force herself to suck in air, to bite back the sound of her gasp.

"Go back to sleep," he repeated softly, as though she were a child who needed to be coaxed to her bed.

But sleep was impossible now. In her dreams she might have conveniently forgotten that Gray had returned to disturb her world, that he had become her neighbor, but now she was wide awake and all too aware of the man. She was also getting another look at that trailer he had rented.

Dragging the sheet close about her, she left the bed and pushed the curtain aside completely.

"Gray?" she finally managed to whisper.

He came closer, near enough that she couldn't avoid looking at him. She tried not to stare at his chest, at the tiny trickle of sweat that streaked down over his nipple, trailing over ridges of muscle to the low-slung band of his shorts where it seeped in.

Quickly she raised her gaze. She tried to look calm.

"Sorry, Cass," he repeated. His voice was a husky caress that seemed to reach underneath the thin sheet that covered her. "I'll have to remember not to take this route down your road in the future. Not everyone gets up as early as I do."

"I do. Usually," she said. "It's just that today is Sunday and I don't have to open the store." *It's just that I didn't sleep well last night.*

"So you and Rob are free today?"

She bit her lip, clutching the loose sheet closer to her. "We have church this morning. I'm pretty fussy about keeping that a family time."

Because she hadn't had that kind of family as a child. And now she was in danger of losing the one she had.

"Mind if I steal some of the rest of the day?"

Yes. Very much so. Gray was a threat to her composure, to her contentment, to her whole world and way of life.

"Mmm, no, o-of course not," she stammered as he raised one dark brow.

"Liar." He reached out as if to touch her through the open window, then brought his hand back to his side. "If you're leaving soon, I'd better let you go. Besides, I need to go get cleaned up myself."

His words brought her back to the subject that had been bothering her ever since she'd glanced across the road.

"I can't believe you seriously mean to stay in that thing." She nodded toward the slightly tilting trailer.

"Cass, you wound me," he teased. "That's my home you're talking about. My castle."

"It tilts." She tried crossing her arms without losing her sheet. "How do you keep from rolling out of bed?"

"Concrete blocks under the end legs of the frame. Works like a charm. Mr. Moser swears by the procedure."

She could tell he was trying to look serious, but his grin was threatening to pop through at any moment.

"Mr. Moser isn't sleeping in that bed, though, is he?"

"No," he agreed. "I can guarantee Mr. Moser was not in that bed last night. I slept alone. Just like you did, Cass."

Her eyes widened, her mouth opened slightly. He slowly placed a hand on the window frame and leaned in. Putting one finger beneath her chin, he tilted her head up so that he was looking down into her eyes, his lips mere inches from her own.

"The trailer is primitive, but it's adequate, Cass." His barely-there touch immobilized her completely. "Just because I'm an Alexander doesn't mean I have to sleep on satin sheets."

His glance strayed down to her body with his words. Her sheet was plain cotton, like the ones she'd always slept on.

Abruptly he pulled his hand from her. "I'd better go get

cleaned up,'' he repeated, turning away in one quick movement, heading for his own side of the road.

She should just let him go. She shouldn't even ask.

''Where?''

He looked over his shoulder, held out one palm as he smiled. ''My host is letting me use his facilities.''

And Gray was probably being charged a small chest of gold for the privilege. But the only other shower in the area was—

She quickly said goodbye and closed the window.

A little guilt was a dangerous thing, she decided later, dropping an egg as she tried to make breakfast. Because only guilt could have made her consider lending her shower to Gray for even one second and she had nearly done just that.

What foolish thing would she be thinking or saying or doing next? Whatever it was, she was darn certain she'd be wearing a lot more clothing the next time she got close to Gray Alexander. She just hoped he would do the same.

The woman had been wearing a sheet.

Gray soaped the sweat from his body, groaning as the hot water sluiced over him. So what if he'd seen evidence of some sort of flowered material under the sheet? No matter that she hadn't been completely naked beneath that thin cotton. The mere way she'd been grasping the material, clutching it close as if he might see something, well...dammit, his imagination had run wild. He'd looked down to where cloth met bare skin and seen...visions he'd stored away for years. Cassie whispering his name as he spread the white cotton edges of her blouse and kissed her breasts, her sweet gasp of shock and need as he slid between her thighs and stroked deep inside her.

''Hell.'' Gray reached for the hot-water knob, turned it until only cold, stinging darts of spray hit his body. He welcomed the icy, desire-drowning droplets.

"Watch it, Alexander," he told himself.

And watch it he would. He'd been halfway to inviting himself along with her and Rob this morning before he stopped himself. Now that he was here, he wanted to speed things up, to make up for lost years. But church was family time, and while Cass and Rob were a family, and he intended for Rob and himself to be a family, those were two separate entities. Escorting them to church would raise eyebrows and trigger questions, and he didn't want anyone asking too many questions of Cass just yet. Not in front of Rob.

There were loads of ready-made problems already floating around, such as how he was going to win over his son—and how he would manage to keep his mind off what lay hidden beneath Cass's clothes. Plenty of potential trouble here.

Gray thought about that trouble as he put the meager contents of the trailer to rights and tried to form a plan for the coming days. He was still pondering the situation when Cass and Rob finally pulled up across the road and climbed from the car. Cass went inside while Rob gave a whistle that brought Bailey running up to meet him. Pulling at the tight cuffs of his shirt sleeves, Rob bent to pet the animal.

"Everything go well at church?" Gray asked, coming up beside his son and cursing himself for his inane question. Why couldn't he think of anything meaningful to say? He who could negotiate a business deal with any smooth-talking competition, looked at his own child and just...froze. It didn't make sense. Or maybe it made too much sense. There was everything at stake here, and this time it was his own backyard that was at risk.

Rob swiveled his head and continued scratching Bailey behind the ears. "Sure. Mom's inside."

"I know. Bet you'll be glad to get out of that shirt and tie. I always was when I was a kid."

Tilting his head, Rob studied him, his brow furrowed.

"Yeah, I don't like wearing this stuff much, but it makes Mom happy," he conceded. Not the kind of thing you'd expect a kid to say. Pride swelled within Gray. The pang at having missed out on watching his child grow to this stage also increased a notch.

When Cass emerged a few seconds later, surprising him, she must have seen the regret written on his face. Gray didn't miss the worried look of apology in her eyes. But of course she said nothing, and neither did he. Rob thought him an old acquaintance come to visit, and Cass wished that was all he was. For now he would play the part.

"Lunchtime, Rob," she said. "Hurry and get changed."

"Wait." Gray's words were for Rob, but it was Cass he looked at. "I... talked to Mr. Moser. He tells me there's a carnival not far from here. I wanted to invite the two of you out. Something simple. Remember?"

Damn, he felt like an insecure kid asking for a date. He could almost feel Cass getting ready to tell him that she had to stay home and wash her hair. She was already fidgeting, her fingers worrying the belt of her slim navy skirt.

But it was his son who shook his head. "I already told Tim I'd come over for lunch and shoot some hoops afterward." Rob scrunched his fingers into the dog's fur and shot nervous glances between his mother and Gray.

"Rob, Mr. Alexander had already invited us out today," Cass chided. "You know that."

"I thought he was just being polite."

"He *was* being polite, and you need to do the same. Go call Tim and—"

"Don't worry, Cass. It's fine," Gray cut in.

She shook her head. "No, it's not I—"

"It's fine, Cass. It's not that big a deal. We'll do something else another day, Rob."

Rob bit his lip, glanced at his mother, then turned to Gray. "I—all right. Sorry about today, Mom. Don't be mad."

Cass opened her mouth, then closed it again. She crossed her arms and looked at her son. ''We'll talk later. And next time, ask first before you commit to Tim.''

''I will,'' he promised, sprinting for the door, already shedding his shirt and tie.

Cass waited until the door had banged shut before she turned to Gray.

''He was wrong. You shouldn't have interfered.''

''I didn't want to force him to do something he didn't want to do.''

Cass leaned back, a half smile of disbelief on her face. ''Welcome to the wonderful world of parenting, Gray. Children don't always want to do the things they should. Sometimes you have to be firm.''

And that was something she'd had to learn all by herself, Gray was sure. Her father had been a poor example of a parent.

''Maybe,'' he agreed. ''But not until Rob knows me better. Not until I can dispel some of that nervous look I seem to inspire in him. Do you think it's the fact that I'm a stranger living in a trailer?''

Cass took a deep breath. ''I think it's more the other—the fact that we once knew each other. He thinks...that is, he's concerned you might want to...to date me. I told him that was absolutely not the case, but—''

''But he has functioning eyes in his head, and he's an intelligent kid who can recognize when a man wants to make a move on a woman.''

Her face slowly slipped into a delicious shade of rose, but she stared straight into his eyes.

''I thought we agreed there wasn't anything between us.''

Gray shook his head slowly, swiping one finger across the frown line between Cass's brows. Her skin was sinfully soft.

''No, I don't remember saying anything like that. We

agreed we weren't a match, but I never said I didn't find you attractive, and there's no point in pretending I don't. There's something...elemental between us, just as there was eleven years ago. If Rob is good with animals, he's probably pretty intuitive. Trying to convince him I'm not drawn to you would only make us both liars, but I'll do my best to assure him I'm not planning on carrying you away over my shoulder."

Cass sucked in a deep shaky breath. "I'm not sure I'd put it that way," she said with an uncertain smile. "At age ten, he just might like to see that kind of stunt."

As if he knew his parents had been talking about him, Rob came out the door at that moment on a run, the laces on his gym shoes still untied and flapping as he ran.

"Be back by dinner, Mom," he called, dashing for his bike. "'Bye." And then as if he knew his mother expected it, he turned for half a second. "'Bye, Mr. Alexander. Sorry again."

And he was gone.

Cass stole a glance at Gray. She suddenly realized she was standing a bit too close. She struggled for something inconsequential to say. "He's normally more polite than that," was all she could come up with.

But Gray put up a hand to halt her. "Don't worry, Cass. I knew this wouldn't be easy. Why would it be? If he's reluctant, I'll just have to go slowly and be more persuasive."

"You have that kind of time?"

Cass couldn't help looking across the road. The trailer sat like a threat in the background. How long would Gray be willing to stay in that kind of enclosure? Any minute he could decide he'd had enough, could tell Rob the damning truth, pack up and go back to Misunderstood, maybe with her son in tow for long periods of time. She swallowed hard.

"All right, Cass. That's it. You've worried enough

about that damned trailer and whether or not I'm going to try to rush things because of it. You're half certain I'm going to drag Rob back to Misunderstood without asking your permission just because I'm staying in temporary and inadequate housing. So, come on. I'll give you the grand tour.''

And without waiting for her response, he closed his big hand around hers and gave a slight tug.

''It's okay. I trust you,'' she said.

''Sure you do. Like a fly trusts a spider.''

Gray kept walking. She kept following.

When they reached the far side of the road and the door of the trailer, Gray stopped. He turned to her.

''Here we go, Cass. Welcome to my house.'' And he flung back the small door.

There was no step and the entranceway was a good two feet off the ground. Without hesitation, Gray reached out and slid a big hand on either side of Cass's waist. For several seconds she felt the warmth of him burning her skin, felt herself being dragged closer as he lifted her and set her back on her feet inside. When he slid his hands away, her sides ached for the loss, but she quickly turned around, moved aside to let him in, and stepped to the far side of the wall.

She cleared her throat. ''It's...much cleaner than I thought it would be. It's—''

''It's not great, but a man could stay here for a while.'' Gray gestured with his hand and she could see he had light, a bit of space and storage, and a bed that took up half the room. It was covered in a white spread. An indentation of Gray's body indicated where he must have lain earlier in the day.

The urge to bolt for the door was tremendous and Cass turned to do just that.

''I can see I was wrong. I'm sorry that I've been so nervous. This is all just so—''

In the small space her hand brushed against him, sending heat throughout her body.

He raised his hand and slid it along her cheek.

"Come closer, Cass," he whispered, slipping his hand beneath her hair. His other arm circled her waist, pulling her close, her breasts brushing against his chest even as his lips came down on her own.

For two seconds her senses whirled and danced in shock and excitement. Then the warmth of his lips against her own, the enticing male taste of him dipped into her consciousness. Cass opened her mouth and the world turned to fire.

She lifted her arms, lifted herself higher against his chest. The warmth and size of him was heavenly. She wanted to be closer, so close her body would fuse to his, so close his heartbeat would become her own. As if a higher power were luring her on, she slid her fingers into his hair and arched forward. She breathed in the scent of his aftershave, of warm male skin.

Years rolled away as he sipped at her, licked her lips, held the weight of her breasts in his hands, his thumbs brushing across the tips.

She was seventeen, wanting and wanton again. The bed was behind her and Gray, and the lure of ecstasy before her.

"Cass." His voice was a promise of release and relief.

"Angel." That one word falling from his lips was a promise of...love.

But that was all wrong. It was what she had once wanted, but what had never been real. This was just...the most basic of drives, sheer naked lust, making them both crazy, making him say...anything, everything. And none of it meant a thing except that there was a burning want here. On both sides.

Gray nuzzled the sensitive skin at her throat, dropped a kiss in the hollow there, seducing her with his heat. His hands teased her flesh and made her want to squirm away from her thoughts, to touch back, to know what she had only known for one night in her life.

A night that had brought pain she never wanted to experience again, she remembered, letting the bitter truth intrude.

"Kiss me, Cass," he said, framing her face with his hands, covering her mouth once again so that it would have been so easy to just...let things happen, to take the mind-numbing pleasure he was offering because she wanted him with a deep, distressing hunger that threatened to consume her.

Except she knew what came after. She remembered what tomorrow promised.

But maybe tomorrow didn't matter.

And maybe it mattered way too much. He was a man who had all and could take all if he wanted. She was a woman who had to make careful choices or risk losing what she had in a quest for what she would never have. Again.

"No," she whispered against his lips, dragging her mouth away, feeling the cold, harsh rush of air as she pulled back.

"No," she repeated as she lowered her arms and gave a slight push against his chest.

Immediately she was free. Her arms were empty.

His eyes were half closed, his breathing as irregular as her own.

For long seconds there was silence. Heavy. Awful.

Gray leaned back against the wall, but didn't look away. He stared straight into her eyes, started to take her hands in his own, then stopped. "I shouldn't have brought you here, Cass. Not for any reason. Not when I've never had a ton of self-control where you're concerned."

She nodded, bit down on her lip.

"You wanted to make a point."

He turned as if she'd slapped him. "Not about this. You think I was trying to entrap you into something you'd made it clear you didn't want?"

"No. You were trying to prove to me that you weren't going to try to drag Rob back to Misunderstood when I wasn't looking, that you were willing to stay and give him time to get to know you, that you could manage to live here for a while. This—" She held out her hands to the walls of the trailer, then wrapped them around her body when she saw that they were shaking. "This was—"

"A man out of control. Nearly lost to his desire."

"I—I guess I didn't help, either," she admitted, knowing that her face was flaming, unwilling to look down to see if all her buttons were fastened.

Gray shook his head, but a small smile lifted his lips. "I'd say you helped a lot, just not in the way that you wanted to. But I'll do my best to keep the lid on my urges in the future, Cass. You're not to worry. Not about this and not about Rob. I'll give him time. As much as I can."

Cass looked at him long and hard, then fled the trailer without waiting for Gray to assist her. The last thing she needed was his hands anywhere near her right now.

"Cass."

She turned to look at him, but continued walking backward.

"I promised you dinner tonight," he reminded her.

Dinner. At a table, her knees nearly touching his.

"That's okay. Really. Another time, all right?" she said, knowing she sounded just like her son. But she couldn't take the words back, couldn't stop. Instead she turned and walked away as quickly as she could, trying to regain the calm she'd learned to treasure these past few years.

But her nerves were spinning. Clearly, she still wanted Gray, and she wanted him gone, as well. But if Gray left, he would make sure that Rob went, too. At least some of the time. She'd lose a part of her son.

''Unacceptable,'' she whispered, entering her house. ''How could you lose it so easily again? And with him?'' And she wondered what could possibly happen next.

The answer came when a truck from Emilio's Restaurant pulled up in front of her house some hours later. A man started unloading clear containers of food. There was a lush green salad, linguine in a thick rich sauce, stuffed mushrooms, and fresh crusty bread. The warm, yeasty scent of the bread filled the air.

''What's this?'' she asked.

He just shrugged and handed her a slip of paper.

I always keep my promises. Gray, the note read. And she knew it was true.

So why did she still feel so scared when Gray had promised to consult her before taking Rob to visit her hometown? He'd promised not to let his passion run wild again.

She should be happy and reassured.

But her dreams that night were of a man whose touch made her cry with longing, a man with chestnut hair who disappeared when she woke in an empty bed and a tangle of sheets.

A man who was truly going to share her son from now on, she finally admitted.

She was going to have to make this work, to become Gray's friend and stop trying to wish him away.

They would get along while they had to. For Rob's sake and for their own sanity. All they had to do was keep things light. Surely she could do that when she had done so many seemingly impossible things in the past ten years.

But another day passed and Rob had proven to be even more elusive than ever. She had been forced to send him to his room for his poor manners, and it was clear things were going to be even more difficult than she had supposed.

''But not impossible, Pratt. Nothing's impossible.''

At least that was what she told herself when she had

paced the floor many times over and finally ended up tentatively knocking on Gray's door later that night.

Footsteps resonated inside the poorly insulated trailer. She stepped away and waited for him a good six feet from the door.

"Cass? Something wrong?" Gray started to step forward. Even in the moonlight she could see his eyes were worried, but Cass held up one hand to signal him to stop.

"No, I'm fine. Really," she said. "I— Thank you for dinner last night. You didn't have to do that."

"I promised."

She took a deep breath, pushed her shoulders back. "And I promised to cooperate with you, too, on this. It's only fair to you and to Rob that I do. So—"

He waited, not pushing or questioning. He just...looked at her and even that was too much, too intense for her. She opened her mouth.

"Rob..." she began, then faltered. She felt exposed by the moonlight, afraid he could read her mind and know she was remembering that kiss they'd shared. But of course he couldn't, and she had come here with good intent.

"Rob frets about his animals," she finally said.

"He takes excellent care of them."

"Yes, he does, but they're definitely his weakness. He's been thinking about asking Jake to help him enlarge one of his pens, but Jake hasn't really been around lately with all the work he's had restoring his house."

"I see."

She hoped he did and wished that she could see his eyes, but he was in shadow, his voice deep and rich in the darkness.

"Does that bother you that Jake hasn't been around?"

Cass blinked, uncertain what he was implying. "I told you he and I are friends. Of course I miss him, but that wasn't the point I was trying to make."

Gray stepped out of the trailer then. He walked into the light and she saw that his hair was tousled as though he had already been in bed. The unexpected urge to smooth it with her fingertips was strong, but she held her hands at her sides.

"You mentioned Jake and Rob's animals because you were trying to help me make a connection to my son. I believe you were trying to do something honorable," he said softly.

His voice mesmerized her. She fought to keep from swaying toward him in the dark.

"Yes."

"But in truth you wish I'd never come here in the first place."

"Yes. I do," she said, her words a bit too emphatic.

He leaned closer then, and she shut her eyes, trying to shut out the effect he was having on her. She felt the brush of fingertips across her brow, her eyelids, her lips.

"Then thank you, Cass. A man would have to be a fool to turn away from that kind of help."

She jerked her head, began to breathe again as he moved away. Turning, she walked awkwardly back to her own side of the road. She had done what she came to do; to make a start on keeping her word and helping her child and his father make a connection. But she wouldn't take a risk like this again. Not in the dark. A woman who came to Gray Alexander in the warm shadows of night and thought she could return home unchanged had to be a fool.

She *would* keep things light, the way she had planned, but that wouldn't be possible in the night when a woman's dreams came out to play. From now on, she and Gray would be friends. Nothing more. Like couples who had worked out an amicable divorce, that would be her and Gray.

The thought enabled her to sleep and to hope. Life could go on, after all.

Chapter Five

"Mind if I help you with that?" Gray went down on one knee in the grass next to his child the next day. Rob had been filling Bailey's bowl, and the dog, excited at the prospect of either mealtime or Rob, had backed into the huge bag of food, sending it spilling.

"That's okay. I'm used to Bailey's spills."

"I'm sure you are, but maybe it wouldn't hurt if I just lent you a hand today."

"No, really. It's okay. I can do it." Rob reached for the bag and sent it toppling again. Gray was pretty sure his child wasn't normally prone to clumsiness. He'd seen him running down the road with infinite grace just the day before.

Gently he reached out and touched Rob's sleeve. "I'm not here to upset you or your world, Rob." Even if that was exactly what he would end up doing.

Rob didn't look up. He continued picking up the spilled food. "I didn't say that. I didn't think—"

"I would never do anything to hurt you or your mother. I don't expect you to know that, since you don't know me, but I'm telling you it's true. I'm hoping you'll believe me."

"You look at her the way John Abbott in the eighth grade looks at Erin Dover. I think you like my mother."

With great effort Gray held back his smile. He wondered if John Abbott knew everyone was watching him make eyes at Erin Dover, but that really wasn't the issue here, was it?

"If you mean that I find your mother attractive, of course I do. She's a mom to you, but almost any man would think that she's a very beautiful lady. If you mean you're worried that I'm going to stick a ring on your mother's finger and move you both to my cabin in Antarctica, then you don't need to worry."

"Would you kiss her?"

Gray studied the question, hoped that honesty was indeed the best policy in this case.

"I might, but lots of people kiss other people without marrying them. I hate to even suggest it, but I'm sure you're going to kiss a lot of girls before you marry one."

Rob's face turned pink. He picked up the food faster. "You wouldn't kiss her if she didn't want you to, would you?"

"Never." The word practically shot out of Gray's mouth with a bit more force than he would have liked. He had indeed kissed her without asking her how she felt about it the other night. The fact that she'd responded, or that he'd stopped when she'd asked him to, didn't change the fact that he had taken advantage of a very handy situation. And he could still taste her, feel her, every time he closed his eyes.

"I wouldn't do that," he promised his child. And he wouldn't. Not again.

"Okay then," Rob answered. "Because Mom told me once that she hoped I didn't mind that she wasn't planning to get married. I figure she probably isn't big on kissing, either."

"And if she did kiss me? Would you make her feel bad about it?"

Rob looked down at his hands. He kept his face turned away and didn't speak for a few seconds. "I made Mom cry once when I was little. She sent me to my room because I did something, and I told her I hated her. She didn't say anything, but I knew she was crying even though she hid in the bathroom. I can't remember ever feeling that bad, so if she wanted to kiss you, I wouldn't say anything to her. But that doesn't mean I'd like it."

"That's an honest answer. Thanks for at least being truthful with me."

When the food was all cleaned up, Rob hoisted the bag and prepared to go, but he glanced at Gray once as if he had something to say. Then he turned and started walking away.

"I never had a pet when I was young," Gray said, stopping his son's movement. "My dad said they were too much trouble and that my time would be better spent on something else. Would you consider... Would you mind if I gave you a hand with your animals now and then? I'm pretty handy with a hammer and nails. I could help you build some bigger shelters for some of them, if that's all right."

Rob's back was rigid, but he slowly turned around. "Mostly I use boxes," he explained. "I'm— I don't know much about making things."

Gray nodded. "Maybe I could teach you then, in exchange for you teaching me about your animals. I might want a pet now that I have time for one. It would be good to know how to be a responsible owner."

Rob sucked in his lip, frowned, then gave a long nod. "Okay. Maybe after lunch then. Is that all right?"

"Yes, that's good." It was more than good, Gray

thought, closing his eyes as his child walked away. It was so much more than good. His son was talking to him at least.

He could make things right...but not really. He could never give Rob a whole, complete family. Cassie didn't want to set things right, the way he'd planned, and he had this damnable urge to slide his hands over her, to feel her lips beneath his every time she came close, something she clearly didn't want to give in to. For once in his life he could not just step in and do what seemed like the right thing. This was more complicated, more dangerous, more scary.

Gray couldn't remember ever feeling more worried in his life—or more alive.

Cass glanced out the window for the umpteenth time and saw the two dark heads huddled together as Gray showed Rob how to measure and cut the wood, how to fit the pieces together to make an enclosure for the animals. For a short time, Rob seemed to have forgotten his distrust of Gray. For this moment, he was almost acting like the son he actually was.

A part of her still wanted to turn the clock back, to do something that would ensure that Gray never found out about Rob's existence. But another part of her was grateful that this connection had been made, so that Rob had someone other than Jake. A real father, even if that father was upsetting her whole life and sense of security right now.

She shoved the last soapy dish underneath the rush of water, emptied the sink and stepped out the door, drying her hands as she went.

"Rob, you've got a game in less than an hour," she said, hating to disturb something that was going so well.

"Yeah, I know. I'm going to get ready." He glanced at Gray as he put his hammer down and started to walk away.

Just before he hit the door, he turned around. "You could come see my Little League game if you're bored. Maybe."

Gray was rising from the ground, and Cass was aware once more of how small he made her feel. He gave her a quick look and she pulled back the door, inviting him inside. What else could she do when her son had just issued an invitation like that?

"No problem?" he asked, following her inside.

Definitely a problem, she wanted to say. Rob would be in the field and she and Gray would be crowded together on a cramped bench. She'd never brought anyone to a game. People would wonder who he was, and who he was, was a man who lived in a world she couldn't even begin to imagine. He was Gray's father, but he had never really been her anything and she didn't want people thinking otherwise. But she had promised herself she'd offer friendship.

"Mom?"

Cass shook her head, somehow managing a smile. "Of course there's no problem," she told Gray. "Not if you don't mind hard benches and overenthusiastic parents."

"Wouldn't miss it," he said, which sent Rob running into his room to suit up.

But once Rob was gone, Gray moved closer. "I'll be minding my manners today, in case you're worried, Cass. Rob asked me to promise not to kiss you if you didn't want it, and I told him I'd do my best to behave myself."

His voice was low, coaxing, teasing, outrageous. His words caught her completely by surprise, threw her off guard, and darn it, she'd been off guard and trying to get her balance ever since he'd pulled up in her yard the other day. It was time to reclaim some of that hard-won self-confidence. So while she wanted to ask him to tell her he hadn't really been negotiating with her son over whether he could kiss her, she resisted temptation.

Instead she lifted her chin, gave a slight smile. "I'm

glad one of us has decided to be smart, Gray, and I promise I'll try real hard not to tempt you in any way, too. I hardly ever kiss men at Little League games anyway."

Gray's grin grew wider. "Hardly ever?"

She raised one shoulder in a very small shrug. "Well, a woman can't be held accountable for her actions if someone on the team hits a grand slam. Then anything goes."

And with that, Cass turned and headed out of the room. Her heartbeat moved into overdrive. Her nervous system did a double take. That whole speech was totally unlike her, but then Gray had always brought out the reckless side of her. Wasn't Rob's very existence proof of that?

"Cass?"

She sucked in a deep drag of air, but didn't turn around. "Yes?"

"Where are you going?"

She didn't know. She was just running from Gray's presence, from the spell he always seemed to cast on her.

"To put on my lipstick," she said, fumbling for a response.

She almost thought she heard a low curse behind her.

"Just in case someone hits a grand slam?" he asked.

Heat climbed up her throat, slid up her cheeks, her forehead. Slowly she turned around. "That almost never happens," she choked out.

"Must be a lot of happy fathers when it does. What shade of lipstick is that, anyway?"

He was almost laughing now, and she couldn't keep from chuckling a little herself. "All right, stop it. You knew I was kidding. I was just mad that you had been discussing kissing me with my son."

And the smile faded from Gray's face. "My son, too, sweetheart."

She sighed, forced herself to ignore his flippant endearment. She nodded. "But that's not the kind of thing I want you to talk about with him."

Gray stepped nearer. He reached out and took one of her hands in his. "Maybe you're right. I don't know much about being a father, yet. But it was something that came up, and he wanted to talk. Maybe the kinds of things he and I talk about won't always be the ones you want us to. Could be different between fathers and sons and mothers and sons. Maybe I'm not the only one learning new things."

He was right. She had no clue what fathers and sons should or did discuss. And maybe she didn't have a right to dictate what they could talk about. In the past few days the number of rights she had was diminishing quickly. And the numbers of fears she had was growing just as fast.

Gray had dropped into her world once and changed it overnight. Now it was happening again. Soon it might be as before. He would come and go and she would be left to learn how to piece her world back together. So what could she do?

Keep it light, she reminded herself, remembering her midnight thoughts last night. Keep it light. Impersonal.

"Let's go to the game," she whispered.

He let go of her hand and stepped back. "Lipstick?"

She shook her head. "I won't need it. Kisses aren't part of my normal activity."

Gray raised one brow at that and she wished she could snatch the words back.

"When was the last time?" he asked.

But Cass quickly moved ahead and out the door. He might choose his topics with Rob, but there were some things she simply wasn't going to discuss.

So she didn't want to tell him when she'd last kissed a man, Gray thought, watching his son sitting in the dugout waiting his turn at bat. True, it was none of his business, but he had a nagging need to know.

And why wasn't kissing a part of her normal activity

when she could make a man moan with just the slightest movements of her lips? She'd been only seventeen when he'd taken her virginity and impregnated her. She'd been growing large with his child when she should have been dating.

Dark anger flooded Gray. Anger at himself, because as thrilled as he was to have Rob and as obvious as it was that Cass loved her child to distraction, the fact still remained that she'd been imprisoned by responsibility at way too young an age. She'd spent her nights tending childhood fears and illnesses at a time when she might have been making a life for herself, having men who treasured, showered her with kisses and slow caresses.

Gray's body went rigid at the thought. He turned to look at Cass, who was doing her best to keep a good six inches of space between their bodies. Pretty tough when the bleachers were creaking with the weight of all the parents here today.

As if she'd felt his eyes on her, she turned his way.

"Rob will be up soon," she told him, nervously starting to lick her lips and then halting the movement as if she knew just what it would do to him. "Are you sure you want to stay through this?"

"You think I don't want to be involved in all aspects of his life?"

She stared, then lifted one shoulder apologetically. "It's not always easy. Like now. Rob...loves playing, but he's not as skilled at baseball as he is at other things. I confess that I chew my fingernails every time he gets up to bat. It's so disappointing for him when he strikes out. It kills me to think I can't protect him from that kind of pain."

Gray stared back, noted her embarrassed blush. "I'm glad you're his mother, Cass. Glad that you care that much. And if it happens, I'll do my best to help you comfort him. You have my word on that. We'll try to minimize any pain."

Without thought he reached out, took her hand as Rob stepped up to bat. He was glad his son hadn't turned to look back at his mother, because heaven knows what Rob would think if he saw the two of them sitting there holding hands.

What he did know was that Cassie's fingers were like ice in spite of the warm day. She was truly nervous. Because of Rob batting or because he had her in his grip?

Maybe both, because as Rob brought the bat around and sliced at air, she clutched his hand more tightly.

He squeezed back. "Easy, love. Easy," he whispered for her ears alone. "He's still got time. Give him time," he said, even though his own heart was racing faster and he could see the worry written on Rob's forehead.

Tugging on his batting helmet, Rob swiped his hand down the leg of his uniform, gripped the bat tighter.

Missed the ball again.

"He's still got another chance," Cassie said. "He can still do it."

But the ball came in too high and Rob moved into a swing he shouldn't have been making. Gray wanted to leap from the benches and run down on the field to help his son, but he forced himself to stay put. He watched as Rob adjusted the angle of the bat, swooped awkwardly at the ball and managed to make contact, dinking it toward the pitcher.

"Go, Rob!" Gray pulled Cassie up by her hand, the bleachers shaking as everyone on the bench cheered his son on. Somehow the pitcher dropped the ball. Somehow Rob managed to slide his foot over the base just before the throw hit the first baseman's mitt.

Letting go of Cass's fingers, Gray looped his arm around her and dragged her close for one quick hug as both of them whooped with the crowd.

When they finally sat down, he turned to her, grinning

like an idiot, he was sure. His arm was still around her. She was smiling back at him, her eyes aglow.

"He did it!" she shrieked. "There for a few seconds I couldn't even breathe. Could you?"

No, she was right. There for a short while he hadn't been able to breathe, and now it was happening again. Because she was breathing very fast right now, her blouse rising and falling with the effort. And she was sitting close against him, thigh to thigh. What's more, she had forgotten to be nervous. For the first time since he'd come back, she was enjoying herself. She wasn't afraid of him. Gray took a long, deep breath and smiled wider.

"Thanks for letting me come with you," he said. "This is the most fun I've had in a long time. But then, I'm pretty new to this kind of thing."

"Fatherhood?"

"Most definitely fatherhood. And Little League."

"Little League? Are you trying to tell me you've never been to a game before? Not ever? How could that happen?"

Cass felt the words pouring from her mouth and knew she was babbling, but she couldn't stop herself. She was so close to Gray right now she could feel the muscles of his leg against her own. His arm was behind her, not wrapped around her shoulder like a lover, but gripping the metal bench just on her other side so that the warmth of his arm was at her back. He was beside her, around her, and his smile—what was he saying? That an Alexander, a man who could buy any entertainment he wanted, was enchanted with the most ordinary of activities? That he'd never even been to a game before?

"You went when you were a kid," she accused, leaning back in disbelief. "You just meant lately, didn't you?"

Gray held up both hands in protest. "Why would I lie? I just...well, let's just say my father felt there were more important activities for me to take part in as a boy."

"What kind?"

But Gray held his answer, held her hand again as the next boy batted and Rob advanced to second base in a torrent of overenthusiastic parental applause.

"What kind?" she asked again.

Gray shrugged as if he was a bit sorry he'd brought up the subject. "Oh, I don't know. My mother—wasn't around when I was a kid, and my father didn't know much about what boys liked to do. He just knew I would inherit the family enterprises when I got older. I spent a lot of time learning things from the ground up."

"That's terrible." Cass was so appalled that a child should have been closed up in dusty offices instead of out running bases that she nearly missed Rob's advance to third.

"Hey, don't look so glum." Gray gently stroked her cheek with his finger. "Smile, don't frown. I liked going to work with my father and uncle. I was good at business even when I was young. Just because I never got around to playing baseball doesn't mean I was deprived. I got out and about, as you well know. It wasn't a hardship. I have no hard feelings."

Maybe not. And of course he was a good businessman. Still...

"Who took care of you when you didn't go to the office?"

He smiled and shook his head. "Playing mother to the world now, Cass? Don't. Not with me. I was a privileged kid who led a privileged life. And I don't look back with any regrets. Well, maybe one," he said sadly.

His eyes were glued on his child. A jolt hit Cass's stomach.

"Do you regret his existence?"

He turned to her suddenly, his eyes dark and fierce. "You know I don't. But I regret...you, what I did to you."

What did he mean? What did that mean? "Then don't," she told him. "Just...enjoy the moment. Please."

Nodding, he turned back to watch the game, but even from the side she could see his frown had turned into a grin. A wide grin.

"Oh, I'm enjoying it, Cass. Loving every minute. Watch this."

She turned back just in time to see that the Elward's son was up with the bases loaded. A long, strong boy, John wasn't the most reliable of hitters, but when he connected as he sometimes did—

Crack! The bat smashed into the hard surface of the ball, fast and strong and sailing out into the outfield, past the centerfielder, past the last blades of grass. The runners loped around the field. Rob looked up and Gray gave him a thumbs up. He answered with an easy, unforced smile.

"He's home and safe, and it's a grand slam, Cass, love," Gray whispered in her ear as the crowd cheered. "Come here."

And in front of God, almost every adult she had regular contact with, and the entire Little League team, Gray kissed her, his lips firm against her own.

"Do you mind if I don't tell them you promised that anything goes?" he murmured against her mouth.

"If you do, I'll—I'll tell Mr. Moser you're an escaped convict, and have him throw you out." She pulled back until she was just a breath away from his lips.

"Then you're not going to kiss all these other men?"

"You knew I wouldn't. And don't laugh at me, either." But she was already starting to chuckle herself.

"I'm not laughing, Cass," he said. "I'm just claiming my prize. Kiss me back."

When he finally released her, Gray turned with a grin to the crowd that was now applauding them. Cassie knew that her face was probably as red as the blouse she was wearing.

"Sorry, folks, but this is sure one exciting game, isn't it?" he declared, managing to look innocent and enthusiastic all at the same time.

In the midst of all the noisy agreement, Cass dared to lean close to Gray. "How are we going to explain this to Rob?"

He raised his brows. "Do you think he'll really expect an explanation, Cass? He looked pretty darn pleased when he stepped on home plate. And you and I...were just celebrating."

And as the game finally ended and Gray jumped off the bleachers and lifted her to the ground, he smiled at her.

"Thanks for having me along, Cass. I guess I never knew what I was missing, and I'm not just talking about that kiss, although that was definitely a very sweet bonus."

"You weren't bored, then?" she teased, knowing the answer already. He had cheered from beginning to end, yelled encouragement and words of consolation to every boy, even the ones on the other team. The parents and team members had smiled at him, warmed to him, and she could see his enthusiasm hadn't been feigned.

"Not a chance." His voice was low, his words meant only for her. "I'm hoping you'll invite me to more games, even after I go back to Misunderstood. Or maybe I'll check out the team in my area and you can come visit me. All right?"

But with his words, the magic left the day. Misunderstood was a different world. There she was the girl who had been thrown out of school, the girl whose father had passed out in the mud too many times. Gray might be a man who took kisses lightly, but if she kissed him in the bleachers there, people would be embarrassed, not pleased. Once he returned home, there would be no shared times like these.

"Here's Rob," she said instead, turning to greet her son. Turning her back on the man who had almost made her forget who she was one more time.

Chapter Six

"Thank you for breakfast."

Cassie hoped she wasn't blushing when she looked up at Gray. There was just something about the quality of his voice, something so firm and masculine and... mesmerizing, and all he had done was thank her for feeding him.

But what else could she have done? Ever since she'd seen how little there was inside that trailer, she'd been fretting. Somehow, on the way home from the game yesterday, she'd found herself inviting Gray for breakfast this morning. Now he was here—close—and she was flitting around like a nervous bumblebee, but she wouldn't have been able to force food past her own lips if she hadn't issued the invitation.

Carefully she picked up his plate and stacked it on the others. "You don't even have a stove, Gray. What have you been doing for the past few days?"

As one corner of his lips lifted, she frowned. "Don't you dare tell me that Mr. Moser is charging you premium prices. I honestly don't understand you two. Is it just because you've got so much money that you don't know anything at all about being frugal or is it that Malcolm Moser is so very good at arguing and it's just easier to go along?"

Gray came around the table and smiled down at her, brushing a smudge of flour from her nose with his finger. "Don't worry about it, angel. But believe me, his cooking isn't nearly as good as yours."

"That's because mine has some real food in it, not just grease. I've tasted Malcolm's cooking, and it would be certifiable homicide to let you continue on that way. I'll send Rob with your meals from now on."

His hand froze in midair, then he brought it down in a slow caress of her cheek. "You don't have to do that, Cass."

It was all she could do to keep from shivering at his touch. "All right, I don't have to, but I want to. I want us to get along. For Rob's sake," she added quickly.

"You'd do anything for him, wouldn't you?" His voice was even lower and deeper than before. "Even make friends with a man you once didn't trust at all."

Cass raised her head, her skin sliding against the cool length of his fingers. She looked into his golden brown eyes.

"How else can we make this work? Don't say marriage," she added quickly.

Gray frowned. He released her from his light grasp. "All right, Cass, we'll be...parents who are friends. You'll cook for me. I'll paint your shutters, fix your flagstones."

"Not necessary."

"Who cares? My son lives in this house, too. And I want to. Let me. I want to."

His words echoed inside her head. *I want to.*

She wondered if those were his thoughts or her own. *I want to.*

And Cass felt herself leaning ever so slightly, anticipating his touch…

Gray groaned low in his throat and took a big step backward. "Better get to work, I guess."

Nodding slowly, Cass knew Gray had just given her a gift of another kind. He'd kept her from making a fool of herself. "Yes. We've both got work."

"Rob and I are making good progress on Bailey's new house. Gonna be a beaut."

An ordinary comment, but one designed to lighten the mood, calm things down, Cass realized. A very good idea.

"I'll bet the Alexander empire's remodeling firm doesn't build a lot of doghouses," she said, playing along.

A gentle smile lifted his lips. "No, you're definitely a special situation."

Yes, she was, Cass thought, watching Gray walk away with swift, long strides. She *was* a special situation. But only because she once had been young and in love and reckless.

Because she'd conceived Gray's child against all odds. That was really the only reason she was being afforded this special treatment, this special time. She had to keep reminding herself of that. Otherwise, she might think those quick casual touches he specialized in really meant something when she knew he was just being…Gray.

"Come on, son," she heard him say to Rob. "Let's get back to work. You're doing a great job." She wondered if he realized that he had called Rob "son" or if it was just a casual term of endearment like the touches he gave to her.

"It's gonna be a beaut, isn't it, Gray?" Rob's words unwittingly echoed his father's, and quick tears came to Cass's eyes. She'd robbed them of this. Of years. Of more.

Now she had to make things work with Gray even if it meant enduring touches that still spun her heart around—and pretending she was totally unaffected by the man.

The ringing of the phone broke into her thoughts, and Cass picked it up, relieved to move on to other less troublesome topics.

"Hello, who is this?" The voice on the other end of the line was elderly...and grumpy...and disturbingly familiar.

"What do you want?" She could barely whisper the words, wondering how much Gray had told his father. Remembering the man's last harsh words of warning to her, she wondered what demands he would make today, what threats he would offer. Did he know about Rob? But no, if that were true, he'd already be here, pounding on the door, demanding things. Hurting people.

"I'm looking for my son, Gray Alexander. This is one of the two numbers he told me he could be reached at. Is he there? And who are you?"

I'm the mother of your grandson. I'm the one who's going to protect him from you. The words formed in her mind, but her vocal cords seemed to be frozen. Her mouth wouldn't move.

"Hello? Who are you? Don't hang up on me, damn it."

Cass took a deep breath.

"I'm sorry. You must have the wrong number," she finally managed to say. And she hung up the phone, staring as if it might leap up and accuse her of being a liar. Reaching for the box where the line entered the wall, she squeezed the clip and disconnected the phone completely. It was a silly thing to do. She would have to put it back soon. But not yet. Not now when the man was probably redialing the number he had just called.

Seconds later she heard the distant buzzing of the portable phone Gray kept in the trailer. Through the open door, she saw him answer it. She knew when he looked her way.

Quickly she reached to straighten an already neat stack of books on a table, hoping a guilty flush couldn't be seen across the distance. She waited for Gray to come over and question her, to ask if his father had called and she had lied to him.

But instead he simply looked her way once more, then went back to working on the doghouse with Rob.

"So have you kissed her yet?"

"The cat? The lizard? Can't see myself puckering up for a lizard, Rob." Gray looked at the tense line of his son's body and wondered if he was making any progress at all. He had thought so, but this…

Rob rolled his eyes. "You know what I mean," Rob said, plopping down next to Gray on the stoop. "Mom's looking funny. You're painting her house. That looks kind of weird to me."

"You're worried."

"Yeah."

"Why? Is it because you don't like me?"

Rob poked his finger into the blue paint around the rim of the can. He looked up into Gray's eyes. "It's not that. We're having fun, you and me. It's just that…Mom's looking funny. Like scared funny."

"And you think I'm the reason?"

"Yeah. No. I don't know. I just don't…like it."

For today anyway, Gray had to admit that he and his child were totally in sync. He didn't like the fact that Cass was acting funny, either.

"I'll tell you what," Gray said. "I'll talk to her, see if there's something bothering her that you and I can do something about. All right?"

"So you don't think it's because you kissed her?"

He wished.

"Not today, Rob."

His son nodded. "Maybe it's just that she doesn't like this shade of blue and she doesn't want to hurt your feelings."

Gray looked down at the bright blue and gave a low

chuckle. "Could be you're right. I got this out of the shed, but maybe we need to pick up something a bit less hard on the eyes. We could get the trim for Bailey's house at the same time." He knew just the special kind Rob would like and he knew where to get it, too.

Rob's eyes lit up. "Bailey's going to have the best house in the county."

"Only the best will do." And that was the truth. Gray was pretty sure no one else would ever have spent this much time building luxury accommodations that were so seldom used, since Bailey had been spending most of his nights in the trailer lately. But this was a special project. For Rob. And for him. This was the beginning of their tomorrows.

"So you'll try to talk to Mom?" his child asked again. "She told me she was just fine."

Gray nodded. "I'll see if we can't do something to bring her smile back."

But when he came up beside her later, she gasped slightly as if her mind had been miles away.

"Let's talk," he said.

She bit her lip, started to open her mouth. In protest, he'd bet.

He touched two fingers to her lips. Such warm, soft lips.

"Shh. I'm not the Spanish Inquisition, you know. I understand why you told my father he had the wrong number."

"He knew who I was?" Her voice was a frantic whisper.

Gray shook his head. "Had no clue. But you can't keep that kind of secret from me, sweetheart. Not with that guilty look that's living in your eyes."

Silence. Two seconds. Three.

"I just couldn't—"

"Shh," he said again. "You don't owe me any explanations. I know your life in Misunderstood wasn't a happy one. I'm sure the ending was even more horrifying than the beginning. You wouldn't want to talk to anyone from there. But, Cass, it's going to happen. More and more, it's going to happen. If you don't go to Misunderstood, Misunderstood is going to come to you, and I'm sorry I'm the one who's bringing this down on your head, but that's as it is. You can be the one who makes the first bold move or you can wait and live your life in fear of the squeaking door and the ringing phone and the unknown car pulling up in the drive."

More silence. Awful silence.

"You're telling me my time is up?"

"I'm telling you that you came here and built yourself a world, fought for your pride and won. You're a strong woman and you've proven it many times over. Don't let an old fear steal that from you."

Cass rubbed her hands over her arms. "What are you proposing, Gray?"

He took a deep breath. "Rob and I need some supplies, some trim David keeps for me at his hardware store. Let me take Rob. Come with us. I promise I won't linger or keep you there too long."

She looked to the side. He could see her agitation in the small pulse leaping at her throat. He wanted nothing more than to take her in his arms, comfort her with his warmth against hers, calm her, protect her. But this time she needed to be clearheaded. She couldn't think straight if he was crawling all over her.

"I don't want to do this, Gray." To her credit, it was a statement, not a plea.

"And I can't force you to. But I think it's time, and I want to take Rob. Just an errand this time, Cass. Just a start. To get past the beginning, all the roadblocks of the first awkward time."

"He wants to?"

"You think I'd bring it up to him without asking you first? I promised I wouldn't. I promised."

And as she raised her lovely blue eyes to him, he saw that he had won. And that she was unhappy.

Gently, he bent down and touched his lips to her forehead.

"Rob's worried about you," he whispered. "Lean on me."

And she did. For ten whole seconds she did, before straightening and pushing back her shoulders.

"Let's make it tomorrow. Let's get this over with."

He nodded and turned to go broach the subject to his son.

"Gray?"

He stopped in his tracks and moved back her way, worrying about her again. Her voice was so small.

She shook her head, held out one hand to fend him off. "I just—we don't have to visit anyone, do we? Not this time. It's too soon. He's—no, *I'm* the one. I'm not ready yet."

And he knew that just walking into that town, just touching her toe over the line, was going to involve a supreme effort, all the pride and courage this lovely lady possessed.

"We'll fly in and out," he promised. "Just going there, just starting is the main thing."

"Yes. We'll start," she agreed weakly. But he knew those words were really a lie. Because the closer he and Rob got to starting their life together, the closer he and Cass were to ending this time they were living right now.

Something painful jabbed inside him at the thought, but then, of course it would. She was an admirable woman. He respected her. He liked her. And of course, as always, he wanted her. Of course he would be bothered for a while when he couldn't see her and touch her every day.

It would end. It would pass. Of course.

But right now he had to think about this business of home, of protecting his son and his—he needed to protect Cass from the past.

The angry buzzing of the alarm clock broke into her dreams and Cass fumbled for the snooze button, intending to grab ten more minutes of rest. But no, there was something wrong, a stillness in the house, a difference, and her "mom alarm" started to ring in her head much louder than a plain old digital ever could.

Grabbing for her robe, stumbling out of bed and down the hall, her suspicions were confirmed. Rob wasn't in his bed.

A quick inspection of the kitchen, the bathroom and the porch didn't turn him up, either.

"Rob." She raced out onto the porch, her feet bare, her robe flapping about her. "Rob!"

He's ten, she told herself. *We live in a safe area. There's nothing wrong. What could be wrong?* But just the fact that she didn't know where he was kept the alarms ringing.

"Rob, where are you?"

And then she saw them, jogging over the rise, Rob pumping his arms, the tall man beside him shortening his stride to accommodate the difference in their reach.

"Hi, Mom," Rob managed to puff out as the two of them came closer. "Did you get my note?"

As if she had been thinking about notes on her mad dash through the house. She'd been thinking of lost children, kidnappers—foolish mother fears—when she should have known there was nothing really wrong. Her child had just gone out for a morning jog with his father. Nothing unusual about that…except for the fact that this was Gray and Rob, and it had never happened before.

"How did you manage to wake him?" she asked Gray. "Once Rob hits the pillow only a major explosion can get him out of bed."

Was that a blush stealing up over Gray's tan cheekbones?

"Actually, I, um, let Bailey whimper outside his window."

Rob's grin was confirmation of this fact. "You know how I am about Bailey, Mom. I don't know what it is but I can always seem to sense when he's nearby and up and about. He's just like an alarm clock. You know what I mean?"

No question she knew what he meant.

"Yeah, Gray says I'm a good runner. Maybe I'll even think about going out for track when I get to junior high."

"I guess Gray told you he was a runner in high school. He was good, too," she volunteered before realizing what words were tumbling out of her mouth.

Jerking her head up, she stared right into Gray's gold-flecked eyes. He was studying her as if he'd never really seen her before, making her feel exposed, vulnerable, too aware of the fact that he was within touching distance.

"I was just okay," he finally said. "But I never knew you went to track meets, Cass. Not a lot of crowds at those events."

She shook her head, suddenly conscious that she was standing here with Gray, dressed in an old, faded bathrobe. Not much had changed, after all, she guessed. Because she hadn't been dressed much more fashionably than this when she had gone to all those track meets, every one she could get to. She had watched, hoping that just once he would look up, see her and smile. Her heart had ached when Andrea Michaels, a cheerleader whose father was a banker, kissed him at the finish line.

"I think I went to one or two."

Gray was still looking at her strangely, examining her, and Cass knew again why she had never even tried to lie in the past. She was just no good at it, felt way too guilty when the false words left her lips.

"We were strangers in the same town. I wish I'd known you better," he said simply, but she was glad that he hadn't. If he'd known he might have seen that their one day together had meant more to her than he'd thought it did. It hadn't been just a young girl's awakening desire.

She shook her head, dismissing the topic.

Because it didn't really matter. That time was better off forgotten. What mattered was that Rob was staring at Gray with something close to admiration. Father and son were building more than just animal houses. They were beginning to build bridges. Little ones, at any rate.

She hoped those bridges held when Rob discovered the truth about Gray.

The thought sent a shiver through her. Gray stepped closer and pulled the edges of her robe more snugly about her.

"We better get your mom inside, Rob. There's a breeze out here." He nodded, sending his child into the house.

But when she turned to follow Rob in, Gray took her icy hand in his own. "I'll be right there with you every step when we drive into town, angel," he told her. "No one's going to call you into the principal's office and make unjust accusations about you this time. No one there has the power to hurt you anymore."

She clenched his hand tightly, grateful for the thought, and managed a half smile for him.

"You're a good man, Gray. You were always a good man."

He was a caring and dutiful man who had lived with power all his life, and he believed he could protect her and Rob, but back in Misunderstood he was still the golden prince and she would always be that worthless Pratt girl whose soul was stained. People had long memories. They would look at Rob and remember he was Cassie Pratt's illegitimate son.

And there was nothing she could do to change that or to protect Rob and Gray from the whispers that had followed her all of her life.

Chapter Seven

Gray could sense the tautness in Cass's body even though he wasn't touching her. Glancing across the car to where she sat, her sunglasses hiding her lovely eyes, he wondered if she was hoping no one would recognize her. If the situation had been less serious he would have smiled at the thought.

"This is probably not a good day to go," she had actually said when they were all finally dressed and fed less than an hour ago.

Immediately Rob's eyes had turned anxious. "But this is the place where Gray lives, and where you used to live, Mom. It's where Jake is, too, and I've never even been there."

"I know that, but..."

Gray hadn't said anything. What could he say without giving secrets away? But he'd reached over and touched her hand, warmed it with his own. To reassure her, he'd told himself, but the silk of her skin made him partially a liar. There was something about her that made him want to touch all the time. It was damn unnerving, this unexplainable need to connect. What did it mean? Nothing. Hell, it didn't mean anything. He was just offering reassurance.

But his good intentions didn't block the guilt when she grasped his fingers as if he were a lifeline. If he was the good man she seemed to think he was, then why had she given birth alone? And why was he putting her through this ordeal today?

Because they were both caught in this trap of lies and mistakes they'd begun a long time ago. And now they had to slowly unravel the web and straighten things out.

"I'm sorry," he said, hoping she knew what he meant.

"No, you're right. It's time."

"We're going?" Rob asked.

She bit her lip and nodded as Gray started up the engine.

Gray had generously headed straight for the hardware store when they'd reached the town, but Cass still couldn't keep her heart from rattling around in her chest. Every rotation of the wheels reminded her of scenes from her past, and she was amazed at how many of them involved the man sitting two feet away from her, his capable hands steering them back into her old world.

"Hey, Gray," a man called as they drove by, and she resisted the urge to shrink down into the seat. That was just curiosity in the man's voice and why shouldn't he be curious? Gray had been engaged a week ago and here he was rolling back into town with a woman and a boy.

When Gray only nodded to the man, Cass closed her eyes in gratitude.

"You're doing fine," he whispered as he parked the car and helped her out. But she wasn't doing fine at all. Her heart was racing, her palms were cold, she felt nausea rising up within her.

"Pratt," she thought she heard someone whisper as they moved to the door, but Gray's body was between her and the unknown person and the sound was too muffled for her to be sure.

"Keep your chin up," he murmured in her ear as they entered the store. "You look lovely, by the way. Did I tell you that today?"

His casual comment when she was feeling like a brittle bit of eggshell caught her off guard. Exactly what he intended, she realized, looking up as he smiled down at her. Because for a few brief seconds, she forgot to shake.

"You're beautiful," he repeated. "Strong. Proud, and rightfully so. Look at him."

And then he was directing her toward Rob whose eyes were lit like ten thousand candles. "He's in hardware heaven," Gray remarked.

"I don't doubt it." She tried to push her edginess aside, knowing she really had no other choice. "He and I don't do the hardware circuit very often."

"It's a toy store," Gray agreed. "Come on."

And moving to join her son, Cassie stepped down the aisle.

"Look at this, Mom," Rob said, holding up a leather tool belt. "Gray's got one just like it."

"Every guy's dream." Gray fitted the belt around his son's hips. "You'll need one of these," he said. "We'll take one home."

"Gray, no, we—" Cass's words froze as she saw a familiar face across the room. Andrea Michaels, former prom queen and girlfriend to Gray was talking with another woman, but staring straight at Cass.

"Cassie Pratt and Jake Walker—" The woman's low words drifted beneath the sound of the ringing cash register and Cass quickly started to turn aside to see if Rob was all right.

"Don't worry, angel," Gray whispered. "He's just down that aisle, so everything's fine. Just try and remember all that backbone you showed me that day I rolled up in your drive, and let's see some now. I'll be right here for you.''

She managed a stiff nod as he positioned himself so she could lean back on him or stand on her own if she wished.

He nodded to the other woman.

''Gray! Oh, Gray,'' The woman's voice was still sexy after all these years, Cassie couldn't help notice.

''Hello, Andrea,'' he drawled.

''Gray, I was so sorry to hear about you and Tess. Still, now maybe you'll have some free time to come visit. I'm so happy you convinced me to let Alexander and Alexander remodel my house. It's been a completely satisfying experience.''

The woman's tone was intimate, and Cassie felt like a store mannequin eavesdropping on a private conversation. She tried to inconspicuously detach herself and head toward Rob, but Gray was in her way.

''I'm glad you're pleased with the work, then, Andrea. You remember Cassandra Pratt, don't you? She wrote for the high school literary journal.''

Cassie lurched and nearly stumbled, but Gray caught her. His warm hand cupped her elbow.

The other woman blinked. A flush rose to her face. ''I—of course, I remember.'' She pasted on a sickly smile as Cass raised her chin and stared straight at her.

''Hello, Andrea. It's very nice to see you again.'' Cass's voice was tight, but she could feel Gray's steely strength at her back, and she held her head high.

''Yes, well, I'd better be going. Stop by anytime, Gray,'' the lady said, heading toward the front of the store.

For long seconds Cass just stood there breathing, the warmth at her back a reassuring haven.

Gray's fingers brushed against her own. ''You were regal,'' he whispered, gifting her with a swift, proud smile when she looked up at him.

She rolled her eyes. ''As if you weren't holding me up.''

"I wasn't. You did it all on your own, sweetheart." Without another word he moved off to find Rob.

She watched the two of them as they ogled various power tools, bits of lumber and lengths of trim. She was sure that while Gray was thoroughly enjoying her son's giddy appraisal of this new world, he was never unaware of her own plight.

Several times she heard her name and instantly he was there, staring at some almost-forgotten familiar face, daring anyone to say anything negative to her, supporting her with his body, with his very being.

People talked to him, warmed to him, swarmed around him as though he had been gone a year instead of a week. The men shook his hand and asked him for advice. The women smiled and flirted and confided in him. This was clearly his domain, his town, but he never seemed to forget Cass was with him. He was always near when she looked up.

Finally he and Rob decided they were done. Cass's legs felt like pudding, but all in all she had survived without too many questions being asked of her. Still, studying the man beside her, something nagged at her. There was one question she wanted to ask.

"Gray?" she whispered as they exited into the parking lot, with Rob running ahead.

"Yes?" And once more, he turned those deep brown eyes on her. She took a deep breath, knowing how all those other women felt, why they flirted.

"How did you know about the writing?" She knew it was a silly question, a little thing, but he had mentioned it as if he had personal knowledge of her that she hadn't been aware of.

He looked to the side, not meeting her eyes.

"You don't think I remembered?"

When she didn't answer, he turned to her and she

couldn't keep from smiling and shaking her head. "I don't think you remembered."

"Why not?"

She shrugged. "Maybe because I almost don't even remember. I only had one poem published the whole time I was in school."

"Okay, you win. Rob showed me."

"Oh, no. He didn't. I'd really rather he hadn't. It was something terribly silly if I remember right." Something Gray had inspired. Something about love.

"It was sweet," he insisted. "He showed me your yearbook photo, too."

She groaned. "If I didn't love him so very much, I'd throttle him right now."

Gray's laugh was deep. He turned and smiled at her. "I'll show you mine."

But she knew what his photo looked like. She'd memorized it years ago.

"Thank you," she said, meaning it. "And not for the photo."

"Was today so awful?"

"No, not as awful as I thought it would be."

"Aren't you glad you came?"

She looked up into his eyes, and knew that this was just the beginning. There would be more trips to Misunderstood. Many more for him and Rob.

Slowly she shook her head. "I can't be glad," she admitted. "But you were right. It was time. I'll be glad someday I'm sure."

When she was old and she had learned to share her son and not want his father. When Gray had married someone else and she had learned to think of him as just an old friend. Then she would be glad.

"It was time to come," she repeated. "Thank you."

"No. Thank you. We can go home now."

Home. *Her* home. His home only for a while. He'd leave

soon. When? Maybe next week. Maybe tomorrow. She didn't know, but she knew it would be soon. Because his home was here, and this had never really been her home, never would be.

But it would be Rob's—part of the time.

She would continue to see Gray—part of the time. For the rest of her life she would see him with her son, with whatever woman he eventually married, and this time there could be no running away from reality.

Cass's hand shook as she moved to the car, feeling Gray close behind her. She would get used to that feeling. She would learn not to react to it.

Soon. She hoped she would learn how to ignore Gray soon.

The woman probably didn't have a clue what she did to faded denim, Gray couldn't help thinking two days later, watching her bend over to pick up the coins her elderly customer had accidentally dropped in the dust.

"Aw, don't do that, Cassie. I was the clumsy old fool that dropped my money."

She gently placed the coins within the clutch of gnarled fingers.

"Everyone drops their change sometime, Bill. It's not clumsiness. The darn stuff just slides away too easily."

Her smile was bright and full of understanding as she looked up at the man whose hands could no longer operate the way he wished they would. She was clearly an angel in disguise as far as this old gentleman was concerned. Gray could tell by the way he smiled on her like a doting father.

She tilted her head and her long braid dipped down the slender line of her spine. The length and sheen and thickness of her hair mesmerized Gray. He remembered that it had been loose around her shoulders the morning he'd inadvertently awakened her by jogging past her window. A tangled shimmer of satin that made a man itch with the need to slide his fingers through it, bury his lips in its softness, breathe in its faint scent of flowers sweetened by rain and sunshine.

"Irrelevant, Alexander. Damn stupid to think that way," he told himself as he watched Cass rise to her feet. No matter how much he wanted to touch and feel and taste this woman, he had to keep the chains on his needs. She didn't really want a physical relationship with him, and in truth, he knew the danger of getting too close to her. Out-of-control desire could lead to other things; emotions, off-limits feelings that could kick the legs right out from under a man and leave him lying on the ground.

"Watch what you're thinking," he told himself, but instead he kept his eyes on Cass, watched *her.*

"Let me just get this last bag of topsoil into your car and then Mary can freshen up her garden when you get home," she was telling the man, moving gracefully toward the awning-covered area where she kept the gardening supplies.

"It doesn't seem right for you to be lifting that when I'm here," the man said, shuffling his feet.

Or when I'm here, Gray thought, putting down the flagstone he'd been setting in the walk leading up to Cass's house. Slowly he started to rise to his feet, angry at himself for daydreaming when the woman was clearly going to take on more than she ought to be handling.

But his movement didn't go unnoticed. It was as if he'd just shot a bullet into Cass's spine. At the slight sound of his shoes on the ground, she froze solid, looked back over her shoulder with a deadly, don't-you-dare look in her eyes.

He took another step.

The anger in her eyes turned to a plea and Gray halted, unable to cross the line she was begging him not to cross.

"Of course it's right for me to be lifting this, Bill," she

said, touching the man's arm lightly. "It's a service I provide for all of my customers. And standing around the store all day, it's just about the only exercise I get. It makes me feel good to be able to know that my customers are getting the best care I can give them. You know what it feels like to do a job well. Every time I look at those picture frames you made for me, I'm aware of how much of yourself you put into them. Would you want someone else doing part of your work for you?"

"You know I don't let anyone go near my workbench," he said as she took a deep breath and let her legs take the weight of the bag she was lifting. Carefully she wrestled it across the yard and into the trunk to join the other three bags already inside. It was a strain. Gray could tell by the way the bag hit the metal, but when she turned she was smiling as though she'd just been lifting feathers.

"Well, there, you see. It means a lot to be able to take care of your own business, doesn't it?"

"Sure does, Cassie," the man said. "And you run a fine store. Mary and I appreciate not having to drive all the way into town for supplies, and nobody else makes a point of asking us if there's anything special we want kept in stock."

Gray didn't fail to note that Cass was walking along with the man as he moved to his car, that she was talking a mile a minute, waving her hands in the air as she spoke. Her customer was so caught up in her cheery voice and her conversation that he probably didn't even notice that she was moving slowly, guarding his steps as he laboriously climbed into his truck.

"Thanks for stopping by, Bill. Don't forget to say hi to Mary for me."

"As if I could forget. As if she'd let me. She's going to want to know how you and Rob are doing as soon as I get through the door."

"Then tell her we're fine. Absolutely fine."

Cass stood there waving as the truck rolled away. As she turned around, the sun lit up her face, which was damp from the exertion of her task. Dark smudges lay on her cheeks where she must have inadvertently brushed her fingers.

Beautiful, Gray thought. Beautiful and giving. She'd made that old man feel young, she'd protected his dignity, cared about him.

"You're very good at that," he told her, slowly walking toward her.

She looked up at him, smiled and shook her head. "I love this store, this place. I like helping my customers. It's not a big store, and it took a long time to even get this far, but I feel a...a connection when I'm able to supply the basic needs of my neighbors."

Gray reached down and took one of her hands in his. Instantly she tried to pull away.

"I'm dirty," she protested.

"Doesn't matter," he said, reaching for the other one, too, coaxing her into his grasp. "And you know darn well you're doing more than supplying the basic needs of people. This isn't just a store. People come here to get their souls stroked. They know that you care about them." The way she cared about her child. And Gray realized suddenly just how important it was that this woman *was* the mother of his child. Because not every woman would care this much, would try this hard. Not every woman would have come to a man and given him tips on how to reach her child when she resented that man's very presence.

Only a very generous, caring woman would do that.

Pride swelled within him. Gently he stroked his thumbs across her palms. He felt the small vibrations move through her body, knew that it would take very little for him to completely give in to everything this woman made him want to do, and quickly and quietly he let his hands fall away.

"Go take a shower now, Cass. Or maybe a bath to soothe those muscles you probably stressed. You should have let me lift those bags for you."

"My job," she protested. "And I can't afford to go inside now. There's no one here to run the store today."

She started to slip around him, to take up her post again.

He slid his hand along her jawline, smoothed his fingertips beneath her hair to the taut nape of her neck.

"I'll watch the store for you. Go," he said. "Your muscles are tight. You need a break," and he gently kneaded the stressed cords of her neck with his fingers to make his point.

She leaned back against his hand for half a second. Less than half. Then she opened her mouth, started to shake her head.

"You don't have to prove your strength to me, sweetheart," he said. "No one else knows how strong you really are, what you're capable of. I know how truly independent you are."

Cass froze beneath his words. Her brow furrowed. "I kept your son from you," she said as if this was a new confession, a penance she had to pay for over and over.

"Worse. You kept your pain from me." And then he made the mistake of looking into those deep blue eyes. They *were* indeed pained, and he kicked himself again for something he could never change because it was long passed away.

"It was my pain. My choice."

She was right, and that thought rankled deep inside him. That she had chosen not to come to him, that she had never felt she could trust him with her concerns or her secrets. That he had somehow been a part of harming her, and he couldn't change that, could never make it up to her. All he could do was take good care of her now, to be trustworthy and honorable and all the things he should have been so long ago.

"Maybe it was your choice, but I'm still sorry that I was ever a part of hurting you." He picked up the thick length of her braid, brought it to his lips and kissed it. "Go inside, now. You're tired," he repeated.

"No, I'm fine." She opened her mouth to say more, determined to prove her independence and strength, to show that she needed and wanted nothing from him, he was sure, and anger poured through him. He reached for her, slid his arms beneath hers, dragged her against his chest, covered her mouth with his own.

Her lips tasted like...Cass, and he knew he'd never tasted anything half as sweet. He also knew somewhere in the back of his mind that he was supposed to ask permission for this pleasure, that he'd made a promise.

"Kiss me, Cass," he whispered against her, and she twined herself about him. The relief was so great that he could barely stand, but nothing could induce him to let go of her now.

Her mouth was warm and soft, the perfect haven for his own lips. He licked at her, ran his tongue along the fullness of her bottom lip, slipped inside as the world around him disappeared in a swirl of sensation.

Cass's fingers were clutched tight against his chest. She moved slightly, unintentionally, and the urge to ask her to do it again almost overwhelmed what little sense he had remaining. He wanted to kiss her forever, to pick her up and seek out a bed. Somewhere. Anywhere. Any kind at all. To have her beneath him and join himself to her in the most ancient ways of men and women.

"Gray. I can't. I can't." The words finally broke through his consciousness and he wondered how long she'd been saying them.

Immediately he let her go, stepped back, tried to find his voice.

"We can't do this again," she was saying, and he knew she was remembering another time, other consequences.

"You're right," he agreed, finally finding his voice. "We're probably the last man and woman on earth who should be making love. I'm sorry I took advantage. I'm sorry I jumped you like that."

Her smile caught him by surprise. "Don't think I'm blaming you, Gray. You were probably just reading my mind, which was totally in the wrong place," she said, shaking her head as a delicious pink glow climbed up her throat and kissed her cheekbones.

Gray held out a hand to halt her thoughts. "You're trying to place some of the blame for this on your own shoulders?"

"You asked me to kiss you," she reminded him. "And I don't recall arguing the matter with you. For a few seconds there, I—I really wasn't thinking very straight. The girls in school were right, I guess, when they said that you really knew how to kiss a woman. You...you do that really well. At least, it seemed that way to me. I don't really have a lot of experience with that kind of thing." And with that, she turned and began to walk away.

Okay, so his mouth was hanging open. All right, so she had caught him totally by surprise. He was even a bit flustered.

"Cassie?" he said in a choked voice.

"Yes, Gray?" She didn't look at him, but she stopped moving away.

"Don't say things like that, all right? About not being able to think straight when I'm kissing you—or about kissing at all. I don't have much faith that I can keep my hands to myself if you do. And Cass?"

"Yes?" She still didn't turn around.

"Are you trying to distract me from my original request? Because if you are—" He reached out again, placed both hands on the curve of her waist, turned her in his arms.

Cass jumped back a good two feet. "All right, I'll go

inside for just a few minutes, but don't think I mean to make a habit of this middle-of-the-day rest stuff. I'm only going inside because my hands are a bit dirty—and because I want to make sure I'm all put together and buttoned up. Can't have the storekeeper looking like she's...like she's just—"

"Been on the receiving end of a man's unbridled lust?" No, they sure as hell couldn't have that, Gray agreed as she moved away. This man had just better keep his hands and his lust to himself from now on. Cassie Pratt might have once been a shy little sweet thing, but womanhood had left its mark. She was ten times stronger now, a hundred times more desirable, a thousand times more dangerous to his self-control when he had exhibited zero self-control the first time they had come together. He, who had spent his life trying to do the right thing and actually succeeding most of the time, was on the verge of doing the wrong thing every time he looked at this lady. And that was just not going to fly.

If he was very smart he would concentrate completely on his son, establish himself as Rob's true father, and end this charade just as quickly as he could and with no ragged edges.

Time to get back to his old practical, unemotional self, and the sooner the better.

Cassie's clothes were rumpled when she woke up. She slid out of bed and realized that the sun had already set. She hadn't meant to take a nap, but when she'd emerged from the shower and sat down to pull her clothes on, the bed had just seemed so inviting. Gray was right about her being tired, even though she hated to admit to a single moment of weakness, but... Gray had been forced to keep watch over her store for much more than the few minutes she had planned.

"That man," she murmured, shoving her feet in her

shoes and heading for the door. A note taped to the screen caught her attention.

"Mom, Gray said it was okay if I ate dinner at Tim's house. I'll see you later. Rob."

Oh no. Dinner. She hadn't even cooked dinner. While customers had come and gone, while the store had been closed, and the dinner hour had flown, she'd been lost to the world. And she had promised Gray she'd make his meals. She hoped he hadn't had to appeal to Mr. Moser for food.

But as she let the door shut behind her all thought of food and Mr. Moser fled. The walkway leading from her house had been finished. She followed the path with her eyes, raised her head...and saw Gray leaning against the fence, staring out across the orchard.

He was still dressed in the jeans and ripped white shirt he'd been wearing earlier. The jeans snugged low at his hips, the shirt clung, outlining his strong, proud back. Turned from her as he was, she could look without worrying about guarding her expression, and she did look, long and hard.

He was magnificent as he had always been, and he was kind, too, she realized. He could have come here and ordered her around. He could have used his wealth to intimidate her, but he had done none of that. Instead he'd gone to great lengths to give her child time to adjust. He'd tried to help her whenever she would allow it. It wasn't his fault, as it had never been, that he was who he was, that he came from a world so different from her own, and that he had to return to that life sometime soon. It wasn't his fault that he desired her with no possibility of there ever being anything more. He was, after all, doing the best that he could, just as she was, and she should be grateful.

She *was* grateful.

"You should have awakened me," she said softly, coming up behind him. And then, taking a deep breath, "Thank you."

"You're welcome, but I'm not sure that letting you sleep was a purely unselfish gesture on my part. I'm not used to vacations. It was good to be making myself useful again."

She nodded, then realized that he couldn't see her, wondering why he still hadn't looked at her. "You missed dinner. I could make you something."

But when she started to move away, he placed his hand on hers, brought it up to rest on the fence near his own. "I'm fine," he told her. "This is beautiful, you know."

Gazing out across the orderly rows of fruit trees, Cass smiled. "You should be here when they're in bloom. It's lovely, but not everyone would see the beauty in an orchard. It's not particularly exotic."

He did turn then, though he kept a good three feet between them. "When I was young, I thought I wanted to be a farmer."

She couldn't help smiling at the thought.

"That would have surprised everyone. I can't imagine an Alexander digging in the dirt for a living."

"Yes, well, my father said something to that effect himself when I told him. The family empire became his world after my mother left, and he excelled at it. It was a world where I felt comfortable, too, but..." He held out one hand toward the land they were discussing. "The orchard was still a nice dream for a boy. There's a certain immediate usefulness that can be rewarding."

"Like building animal enclosures, painting fences and fixing walkways?"

He shrugged. "Don't get all huffy about those things, Cass. They needed doing. I had the time."

She leaned her hips back against the fence, looked straight up into his eyes. "I'm sorry if I've been stiff and unbendable about accepting your help. It's true that I'm not used to assistance, but that's no excuse for being ungracious. I appreciate what you've done here and how patient you've been."

He turned his attention to her fully then, and she could see the dangerous golden glints in his eyes. "There's a limit to my patience, though, Cass. And I mean that in more than one way. I think you understand that. We're going to have to take this into the next realm soon. Very soon."

His gaze held her own as clouds slipped past overhead in the darkening sky. For seconds, long seconds, they studied each other, and she couldn't have looked away even if a cloud had fallen and crashed down on her. From the moment she'd first met this man he had represented a danger to her, a real risk, but that wasn't his fault any more than it was hers. And he was right. They didn't have a choice here. A dangerous liaison was not an option when two people shared a child.

"Soon," she promised. "We'll tell him soon."

It was apparently enough. He nodded and even smiled a bit. "What did you want to be when you grew up, Cass? Did you have any dreams of your own?"

Yes. She had wanted to be a princess. His princess. And that dream had been no more practical than his own.

"I wanted to be a ballerina," she said with a quick grin. "But considering the fact that I'm a terrible dancer, I can't imagine why."

He curved up one corner of his lips in a look of disbelief. "You're a very graceful woman."

"Only if there aren't any other toes in my vicinity."

"No dancing lessons?"

She opened her mouth, then closed it again. Dancing lessons hadn't been an option in her family, but she didn't want to make him uncomfortable by saying so.

"I didn't have time."

But he'd apparently had time to think and to realize his mistake.

"There's time tonight. Dance with me?"

He held out his arms.

She hesitated.

He understood. "It's a risk, I'll guarantee you, but one I think we need to get past. If we're going to grow old running into one another time and time again, we need to learn how to interact and yet be impersonal. Someday we'll probably dance together at our son's wedding. Trust me, Cass. Teach me to trust myself."

And so she moved into his arms. He grasped her lightly, held her at a distance.

The feeling was wonderful…and frightening. The urge to step in close and ask for his lips on hers again was so tempting. But she couldn't. It was wrong, it would hurt so many people, and besides, he had asked for her to help him. She closed her mind and glided in his arms over the grass.

His hands shook just a bit and she knew he was fighting the feeling, too, but he stiffened his fingers. He looked past her into the night.

Want and need and so much more battered at her heart, her mind. Cass closed her eyes and tried to just concentrate on the exquisite movement of this moment with Gray, of knowing that this moment would be one of the few when they could ever really touch again.

"You're a wonderful dancer," he whispered, his voice thick and choked.

"It's you," she couldn't help whispering back. "You're doing all the work."

"I'm fighting every urge in my body."

"Me, too."

"Thank God. Don't stop fighting. Don't let me touch you."

Silence surrounded them. The clouds darkened and rolled past.

Cass wanted to stop, hoping that the ache would stop with her. She wanted to dance with him forever and never have to face anything but his arms.

By the time the first roll of thunder reached her ears, Cass felt like an old rag doll. Worn out and shaky and limp.

Gray stopped moving. He placed her away from him.

"Thank you," he told her. "I'd better go get Rob. We don't want him to be away if there's a storm."

Cass raised grateful eyes to his as he led her to her door and rode away to save his child from the wind and rain.

"I'll tell him soon," she promised underneath her breath. Gray had been patient, far more patient than most men would have been, and he was in an intolerable position right now. She was keeping him away from the home and work he loved, keeping him from his full rights as a father. She would have to make the move soon.

There would be no more dances with Gray. This time with him had been a gift of sorts, but it was ending fast.

She had to take the next step and end it completely.

Chapter Eight

"It's raining pretty hard, isn't it, Mom?"

Cassie nodded as she gave Rob a hug and herded him off to bed. She knew what he was thinking because she'd seen him looking out the window. She was thinking the same thing herself. The trailer didn't look like a very secure shelter against a downpour.

But there was nothing she could do right now. What could she do?

"Do you think he's all right?" Her son's voice came out of the darkness and she bent closer.

She didn't know. She wanted to hope everything was fine, to tell herself the trailer had no leaks, but all she could remember was that there was little room to hide in the small, tight space. The bed took up most of the room and would soon be soaked if the water came in. Gray had no containers to even catch the stuff since there wasn't a stove or sink in the place. But Rob would just worry if she told him that. Why should more than one person lie awake worrying tonight?

"He's probably fine," she managed to say, trying to

convince herself she could make her statement fact just by repeating it often enough.

Rob braced himself on the pillows, half sitting up. "Do you really think so? He wouldn't even keep Bailey with him tonight. He made me bring him inside."

So much for pretending there was no problem. Cass stared at his worried eyes and knew that whether he realized it or not, his concerns had a firm foundation. If Gray wouldn't let the dog stay in the trailer there was a reason. The man was no doubt lying in a wet bed right now and what was she going to do about it? Ignore that fact? Go to bed and leave him that way? Pretend everything was all right?

"He's probably fine," she repeated, "but I'll take an umbrella and go see about him, just to make sure. All right?"

She saw the shadowy movement that signified his nod. "Be careful. It sounds windy out there."

Yes, it did. Just one more reason why Gray shouldn't be staying in that darned tilting trailer. Sharp anger welled up in Cass, and she knew it was more at herself than at Gray. Because she'd been putting off the inevitable and she should already have taken care of things. Of course it was going to rain sooner or later. It was way past time to bring Gray fully into his child's life, and she'd just been avoiding the issue. She didn't want to think about her reasons.

The door was nearly wrenched out of her hands when she opened it. There was no point in taking an umbrella, after all. The wind would turn one inside out in no time. Instead she slipped into a raincoat, lowered her face against the wind and ran out into the night. There were plenty of towels to dry off with when she returned.

"Gray!" she called, banging on the door when she reached the trailer. "Gray! It's Cass." She beat on the metal with her fist and nearly fell inside when it suddenly swung open.

"What the—Cass, what are you doing outside? Come in."

But she remembered all too well what had happened the last time she'd been alone with him in this closetlike space, and he was standing before her now, his shirt hanging open, his jeans open a notch at the waist. She'd already reached her limits in his arms once today.

"Your roof is leaking," she said instead, letting the rain pour down her face. "You can't sleep here."

"And you can't stand there much longer." He pulled her into the trailer, which was leaking all around them, but at least the downpour inside was a bit less frenzied. She looked at the chair where he had dragged a blanket and pillow.

"You could have come and asked for shelter," she accused.

But she knew he would never have done that. She had made rules when he first arrived and he would never have overstepped the boundaries.

"I don't think it would be wise for you and I to share a house, Cass. Not one that cozy."

"You're right. It's not wise, but it's the way it has to be," she said, tugging on his hand. "The wind is gusting too much tonight. This isn't safe."

"You and I under one roof isn't particularly safe, either," he reminded her. "I only have so much willpower, Cass."

She nodded. "I'll try to help, but you have to come now. I won't sleep tonight if you stay here," she said, and he sucked in his breath slightly.

"Rob's worried, too," she told him. "Come with me."

And this time he followed her, curling himself close to protect her from the wind and rain as much as he could in the short run back to the house.

Inside, they pushed the door shut and stood dripping on the tile just inside the entrance. Gray's shirt was molded to his chest. Droplets of water were caught in the curls there.

Cassie felt the old, familiar feeling, the wanting and knowing she couldn't touch. No matter. There was no choice here. He had told her she was strong. She would just have to be even stronger.

"I'll get some towels," she offered, rushing forward and putting some space between them.

"Mom?" Rob's voice called as she passed his room.

She stopped in the doorway. "Gray's here for the night. Do you think you can sleep now?" she asked.

"Now I can," he said, and she could already hear the sound of drowsy relief tinging his voice. "G'night Gray," he called out.

"Good night, son." Gray's voice was laced with love, and Cass shoved the towel up over her mouth. Rob was Gray's son, not just in name now, but in affection. She was cheating both of them by concealing the facts any longer. It was time to pull the man deeper into his son's life, to get rid of that dratted trailer and to face the horrifying fact.

She had been lying to her child for long, long years and now she was going to have to tell him so.

Forcing her steps back to the front of the house, she handed the oversize towel to Gray. His fingers brushed her own, he looked down into her eyes.

"What do you think he'll say when he knows?" she asked, and wished her voice were firmer. "What would you say if your mother told you she'd lied to you all your life?"

His hand clenched over her own, a sudden convulsive movement, and she remembered what he'd said about his mother leaving his father. She realized he must have been very young when that happened. It had been before she and her family had shuffled into town.

"I'm sorry," she said simply. "I didn't think."

Gray shook his head. "It wasn't the same. Rob knows you love him."

"I'm sorry," she said again. "He cares for you. I know he does. I should have told him a long time ago."

"You thought I wouldn't want him. Anyone would have done the same."

Maybe not, but thinking back, Cass knew *she* would have done the same. This was a complex matter, but she couldn't expect a ten-year-old boy to see things that way. And she couldn't stand here shaking, holding on to Gray's hands all night.

"Let me find you some bedding," she told him.

"All right." But he pulled her close and held her, wrapped the length of his warm arms around her. She let him. For now she needed this. She wanted it.

"We'll make it right," he promised, and she knew he meant to try. He was a man who had spent his life making things right. She was glad he and Rob were going to finally come together, but she knew her child well. Things were not going to be right come morning.

And in no time at all she wouldn't have the luxury of Gray's arms for comfort. She couldn't get used to leaning on him...and so, taking a deep breath, she pushed away. She kept her thoughts at bay by opening the sleeper sofa and making a bed for Gray.

"We'll work it out, Cass," he promised again. "Try to sleep."

"Will you be sleeping?"

"With you just one room away and the prospect of claiming my son tomorrow? What do you think?"

She thought the night would be long. She thought her life had been irrevocably changed by this man and would never be the same again.

* * *

''Rob, wait. Don't go yet. Gray and I have something we need to talk to you about.''

Gray sat in the kitchen the next morning looking at Cassie's ashen face, the taut line of her lips. He saw that Rob had noticed the change in her, too.

''Mom?'' The slight quiver was unmistakable even though Rob tried to clear his throat and try again. Automatically Gray reached out to him just as Cass did. Their hands met over his, and Gray gave way, letting her take the lead. Still, he was determined to help her. He wasn't going to let her take all the blame when he knew in his heart he was clearly to blame somehow for much of this. He wasn't sure of the details but he knew he had failed her once. He damn well wouldn't do it again.

Cass glanced his way just for a second. Worry was written all over her face, but she took a deep breath and turned to her son.

''Rob,'' she said, her voice quivering just a touch. ''I have to tell you something and—it's something that's really…difficult. You know how I've always said that your father couldn't be with you?''

Rob's eyes widened. He took a long, deep breath.

''I know that, Mom. I told you I wouldn't trade you for any old dad, didn't I? Is that why you're looking like that, because I've been hanging around with Gray and you think I'm really wanting a dad badly?''

She shook her head hard. Her blue eyes misted over, and she grasped her child's hand more tightly.

''I know you love me, Rob, and I love you, too. More than anything. But, Rob, you did actually have a father. You do, and it seems I—I have to tell you he didn't know about you when you were born.''

Rob swallowed hard. He pulled his hand out from under Cass's. ''He didn't even know I was born? How come he didn't know that, Mom? Was he—somewhere you couldn't find him? Somewhere you couldn't tell him?''

But in spite of Rob's words he was looking at Gray. Hard. He swallowed again, then turned quickly to his mother. ''Mom?''

Cass bit down on her lip. ''He didn't know, Rob, because I didn't tell him. It's very hard to explain, but I thought—at the time I thought—''

As if she didn't even realize what she was doing, Cass opened her fingers, reached out in Gray's direction.

''Your mother had good reason to think I wouldn't want you. I had told her I didn't want children.'' Gray enfolded Cassie's hand in his own even as he turned to his son.

Rob stood up suddenly. His chair crashed to the floor with the sudden, jerking movement. ''You're my father?''

And as if the last few days had never happened, as if no connection had ever been made, dark anger filled his child's eyes.

''You're my father? You didn't want me?''

''He didn't know about you, Rob.'' Cass stood, circling the table, holding out her arms to comfort her son, but he jerked away. ''When he finally found out, he came.''

''But you didn't say anything. Nobody said anything.''

''That wasn't your mother's fault. I wanted you to get to know me before I dropped something like that on you.''

Cassie opened her mouth and Gray knew she was going to take her share of the blame for that fact, but that wouldn't serve any purpose. Rob was treading deep emotional water as it was.

''You should have told me,'' Rob shouted, crying now as he stepped away from his mother. ''He was close all along and you should have said so. You never said so. I thought he was just an old friend. That's what you said. He was a friend. And I believed you. I always believed you.''

The door bounced and banged as he ran from the house and fled.

"Rob!" Cass started toward the door, but Gray grabbed her, held her back against his body, hung on until she finally slumped forward, limp and defeated.

"Cass?" He ran his hands down her arms. "Give him time, Cass. You're his mother, his anchor, and he loves you. He'll remember that soon. He'll need you then." Gray hoped against hope that his words were true. What had he done on that day eleven years ago when he had told Cassie Pratt that he didn't want to be a father? And what had he accomplished by invading her life now? He prayed he hadn't hurt this woman and this child in ways that couldn't be mended.

But she didn't answer him. Instead she pulled away and moved to her room, closing the door behind her.

Gray stared after her for long seconds before going outside. Well away from the house, Rob was on his knees, his body trembling, his arms locked tight around Bailey's thick, furry neck.

Slowly, Gray began to walk toward the boy and his dog. He wanted nothing more than to shield and offer comfort, but when he got within hearing range, Rob looked up.

And then his child ran. Hard and fast and furious, with the dog bounding beside him.

Gray Alexander had finally come to claim his son and he was ten years too late.

It was worse than she had ever dreamed it would be. She had hurt everyone much more than she had even imagined.

Cass watched her normally happy son vanish as though he had never existed. She was watching him out the window and she saw when Gray had tried to go to him, saw Rob run from his father. Pain had radiated from Gray as he stood there alone.

She had kept them apart for all these years, and now they were both struggling with a truth neither of them had expected. Only she had known. She could have prevented this.

Her son would never again have that childlike trust and innocence that had lived within him all his life. How could she forgive herself for stealing that away from him? How could he ever forgive her?

"Cass?"

Gray's voice was soothing, worried, and hot tears rushed to her throat, filled it completely. She couldn't turn, couldn't look at him, couldn't speak. Instead she concentrated on simply breathing in and out, on not crumpling to the floor. She wanted to say she was sorry, but sorry was much too small a word for what she was feeling. It couldn't even begin to speak of her regret.

Cass opened her mouth, then shut it quickly, trapping the sobs that threatened to spill over.

"Cass, talk to me."

His footsteps behind her were as dear as a kiss. He was going to offer her comfort, to touch her somehow, maybe to wrap his arms around her. Of course he was. Gray Alexander couldn't breathe without caring about others' pain, but she had hurt him so, wronged him so, and she didn't deserve his comfort or his concern. Not in this lifetime.

Gray moved closer.

Cass fought her selfish need for him. She stiffened, gave a small, jerky shake of her head and moved away from his inevitable touch.

For long moments she felt him behind her, though he came no closer. And then she heard him move away. The door closed.

I'm sorry. She mouthed the words, stuffing her fist into her mouth to stifle the sound of her sobbing speech. "I'm sorry I loved you. I'm sorry I stole your son from you."

Hours later she rose from the bed where she had finally

fallen. She rebraided her hair, went into the bathroom and washed her pale face. She had given Rob some time alone, time she was sure he had needed, but she had to go to him now, to offer as much love as he would accept. She also had to face Gray now that she was able to stand on her feet without wobbling, now that she could apologize to him without breaking completely apart.

Her child was right where she expected him to be, close up against Bailey, sitting on the porch surrounded by his animals.

Cassie sat down a few feet away from him. He turned his face from hers.

"Rob, I'm sorry," she began. "I love you more than I can ever tell you and I would never intentionally hurt you. Not ever. You have to believe that."

He turned his face farther away.

"I don't want a father. I never wanted one. We were happy. You shouldn't have let him come. You should have told me." Rob hid his face in Bailey's side, and Cass could see he was struggling not to cry.

She reached out, touched his hair, remembered how his troubles had once been small things she could simply kiss away. Or sing away. Or rock away. She longed to pull him close right now, but he had already jerked away from her hand.

"He cares about you, Rob. And I love you, sweetheart. So much. I'm…so sorry."

But Rob had pulled even farther away. He was practically pushing Bailey across the porch, trying to make his escape.

"I don't believe you. He came here to see you, and you never said. You never even said. Neither of you. He came here to see *you.*"

"No."

"Yes, he did. He didn't want kids. You didn't tell him."

He was sobbing now. Wildly, his fingers digging ruts in

the big dog's fur, his tears falling freely. But when Cassie tried to hold him, to comfort him, he curled into a tight ball, stiffening his body, locking her out.

Afraid to leave him like this, she tried to soothe him, stroking his hair, smoothing her hand over his small, shaking back, whispering her sorrow and her apologies. But he never uncurled. He never spoke to her again.

Eventually his sobs turned to soft breathing, and she gently placed a blanket over him and the dog he still clung to.

Cass lay down beside him, wishing she could have done something differently and not knowing what that something was. The past couldn't be changed. Only the future could. She just hoped that when Gray went home, he would be content with small bits of Rob's time, and that she could learn to shut down her emotions where Gray was concerned. She would. For Rob and Gray's sake, she would have to do that.

If he'd stayed away, Cass and Rob would still be happy now. Gray stared at the woman and the child sleeping on the bare wooden floor of the porch. Even in the moonlight, he could see the tear tracks on his son's face. He knew Cassie's sleep was fitful. Her hands were clenched. Her beautiful forehead was furrowed.

Maybe he should have stayed away…but how could he have done that? He couldn't have, and he wasn't really sorry that he had come. Only sorry that he'd brought so much pain to this woman, this child.

Bending, Gray gently lifted his child into his arms and carried him to his bed. He was a handful, no mere babe. All that was long past. But he was precious, so very precious, and Gray dropped a kiss on his son's forehead as he slid him between the sheets.

Rob stirred. He opened his eyes in the moonlit darkness.

And then he saw where he was and who was with him and he stiffened. He tried to climb from the bed.

"Don't do that," Gray said. "Running isn't going to change things."

"I don't—I don't have to listen to you," Rob said in a small voice. "You're not—really my father. You haven't been here all this time."

Gray closed his eyes. He took a deep breath. "I'm here now, Rob. I came as soon as I knew. I wanted—I want to be your father."

"Mom didn't say." Rob's voice was climbing higher, getting hiccupy. "Why didn't Mom say? Why did she lie? I hate her."

Gray swallowed hard to keep his own tears in check. "Don't hate her, son. She loves you."

"Noo-oo." Rob's voice was a wail. "She lied."

Sitting on the bed, Gray caught him close. "She—had her reasons. I can't explain, but I know your mom's life was hard when she was young, and she *did* think I wouldn't want you. She was trying to protect you from knowing that somehow. She was afraid you would be hurt if you knew who I was and I never came around, and she never, ever, expected me to show up like this. And as for her not loving you, you couldn't be more wrong. Didn't she make a home here just for you? Of course she did. You're her world, son, and I'm sure she spent a lot of nights taking care of you when you were sick and a whole lot more nights worrying about you when you were hurt or upset about something. It must be very hard to be a mom all alone."

"Sometimes Jake was here."

Rob's voice was scratchy, but his tears were slowing. Gray tried not to think about Jake being the father Rob had wanted all along.

"Your mom is worried about you." Gray spoke softly. "Because she couldn't keep you from being hurt. She's been crying this afternoon and right now she's sleeping out on the porch because she didn't want you to be all alone out there.''

Rob was silent for a few minutes. ''Does she have a blanket?''

Gray shook his head. ''I was going to put her in bed as soon as I tucked you in.''

Another five seconds of silence. ''I don't like making Mom cry, but—''

''She would never have purposely hurt you, son.''

Rob nodded slightly. ''You've been doing lots of stuff for Mom. Painting and fixing the walk. I thought you were just keeping busy while you were here, but...did you come here to marry her?''

There was no eagerness in Rob's voice and Gray knew what his child was thinking. ''I came to see you, Rob. I came because I wanted you to be my son as soon as I knew you were alive.''

He looked right into his child's deep blue eyes. Imperceptibly Rob moved closer.

''Mom's probably cold.''

Gray nodded. ''We should put her to bed, shouldn't we?''

''I don't want her to be cold.'' Rob crawled from his bed and reached out his hand to his father. When Gray grasped it, he noticed a tear tracking down his child's cheek.

''Rob?'' he asked, brushing the tear away with his thumb.

''I don't like it when Mom cries,'' was all his child said, and Gray gathered him into his arms.

''She was worried about you,'' Gray said. ''But that's what moms do, I think. Are you going to be all right tonight?''

Rob's nod was small, barely visible. He was still way too pale, and Gray wondered how long it would take his son to adjust to this sudden change in his life. He wanted to know if Rob had secretly wished all along that Jake was really his father, but it wouldn't be fair to Rob to ask that question when there really was no choice left after all.

Cassie woke to the feel of a man's warm arms around her. Her feet were dangling and her head was resting on Gray's shoulder. She didn't want to move...until she remembered all that had happened in the last few hours.

"Gray, what's happened? Is Rob all right?" She sat bolt upright in his arms, nearly pitching forward out of his grasp.

"Shh, be still," he told her quietly. "Rob's here."

"I'm sorry I was mean to you, Mom." A little voice at her elbow had her leaning over Gray's arm to look right into the eyes of her child.

Tears filled her eyes and two trickled down her cheek.

"Rob, sweetheart, don't be sorry for anything. Mom's the one who's sorry. I should have told you...something years ago."

"You're crying."

"I'm just happy we're talking again. I love you, sweetheart. Put me down, Gray."

But Gray was already depositing her on her bed. Cassie struggled up to her elbows and reached out to her child. She soothed the hair back from his brow and he didn't jerk away. There was still a wary light in his eyes, and she hoped it would fade in time, but for now she was just grateful for whatever miracle Gray had wrought.

"You're not going to cry any more, are you, Mom?"

She smiled and shook her head, running her hand down his cheek. His blue eyes were red-rimmed and tired.

"Get some rest," she soothed. "Things will work out. We'll talk more tomorrow, okay?" She leaned over and kissed him on the cheek.

He didn't wipe it off in the silly way he always did, and

he didn't kiss her back, either, the way he sometimes did. But he stopped to look at her just before he went out the door. He had at least stopped running.

"Good night, sweetheart." Cassie watched as her child wandered off to his own room.

"I owe you a thousand thanks, and a million apologies," she told the man standing beside her bed.

But his face was stern, set in stone. "I shouldn't have come back and done this to you," he said. "I wanted to hurt you when I first arrived and it seems I've done just that. I've hurt Rob, as well."

"No." Cassie planted her hands on the bed and rose to her feet. "No, you didn't."

When he started to speak, she reached up and placed her fingertips lightly over his lips.

"Gray, I've always taught Rob that it's important to tell the truth, but I deliberately hid it from you and from him for years. You had every right to be angry with me, and I'm the one who really hurt Rob. I never thought I could. I thought I'd die before I brought him pain, but today—" Cass broke off. She shook her head when Gray came closer.

"Sweetheart. Cass. Don't be sad."

She let her shoulders sag. "Can't you just once stop being so nice? Why don't you yell at me? I deserve it. I wish you would." Two more tears slid from beneath her long lashes.

But Gray had come up in front of her now. He slid his hands up behind her back, drew her close even as he walked her backward.

"Don't do that, sweetheart. Please. Rob is right when he says it's awful to see you cry. Maybe it's because you spend so much time trying to be strong that we know you have to be hurting a great deal to shed tears."

He stepped closer, leaned lower. Her eyes drifted closed as he dropped a kiss on each eyelid.

He stroked her tears away with his fingertips and kissed the wetness of her cheeks.

"Gray, don't comfort me." Her voice was a soft wail, which he swallowed when his lips came down on hers.

"Shh, love," he whispered against her mouth. "Things will be all right. They will. Don't worry."

But as he ended the kiss, pulled back the covers and picked her up and tucked her into bed, Cass knew he was wrong.

That kiss had not been born of passion like all the others they had shared, but the tenderness of it was twice as devastating, much more alarming.

She might not be a tearful woman most of the time, but the day was coming soon when she would cry again—every time she remembered that kiss and thought of Gray for all the rest of the years of her life.

Chapter Nine

Gray carefully put the telephone receiver back in its cradle. He stared across the blue and white kitchen to where Cass was cooking eggs, her back turned toward him.

She had answered the phone. Her voice had been strained when she handed it to him.

"I'm needed at home," he told her quietly. "I'd like Rob to come with me for a short time."

She whirled around, her fingers gripping the spatula so hard that her knuckles stretched the skin. "No," was clearly on her lips, but she didn't voice the word.

"Why now? It's only been two days since we told Rob..."

He crossed to her side, gently pried the utensil from her fingers. Her skin was cold and he warmed it with his own, brought her hand close to his lips.

"I would have had to leave soon, anyway, Cass. We both knew that. I've delegated most of my responsibilities, but while my father doesn't get out much and was thrilled to handle some of the business again, he's not able to do it all."

Huge blue eyes stared back at him. Frightened eyes, but steady. Cassie had been pushed to the wall over and over in the past two weeks and now he was pushing her again. Without any real warning. And she still hadn't said yes.

"You haven't had much time to adjust to each other yet," she said. "Rob's still getting used to the reality of having a father. I thought you might like to wait just a bit..."

"I'd like that, Cass." Gray knew he'd never meant anything more. He had come here prepared to hate her, to rip his child from her, but there was something about the lady—if things hadn't changed in the last few minutes, he wouldn't have wanted to leave. Not just yet, but...

"My father's taken ill, Cass. I didn't want to tell you and make it seem like I was making a sympathy bid for Rob, but—"

She closed her eyes. Her hands clenched his own.

"I'll talk to Rob." She stepped back. "I'll ask him. I'll explain."

He caught her hand as she slid away. "I would have done this differently if there had been time," he said.

"I know you would have," she whispered.

After Gray had left the room, Cassie pressed both her hands to her heart, trying to still its heavy pounding. Fear, dark and threatening, pushed at her. This was too soon after all the upheaval of the past few days. Hugh Alexander sick? It hardly seemed possible that such a powerful man could ever be weak, but she knew it was so. Gray's eyes had revealed his concern.

And Rob? Rob was just starting to get past her deception. He was vulnerable right now. If he went away with things still so raw and unsettled—no, she didn't want that. More than that, she didn't want to think about where all this might end. What would happen when Hugh met his grandson? Would the man be happy to see him? Would he try to stop her from bringing him home? Or maybe he would hate him, hurt him somehow.

And what if she simply said no? The thought nagged at her as Cass moved to the back of the house where she could hear Rob cooing to his creatures.

"Rob, I need to talk to you."

He turned to her with a soft smile in his eyes. And she knew that "no" wasn't a possibility. No more secrets. She'd learned her lesson. Rob had a grandfather, one who was sick and old. Maybe not a loving man, but Gray's father nonetheless. If her child wanted to meet him, then he had the right. If Gray wanted his son to visit him, she wouldn't stop Rob from going. And if it felt as though her heart was leaving her body when the two of them drove away, what then?

Then she would have to deal with it, she told herself as she explained to Rob that he'd been invited to Misunderstood.

The couch where Cass had invited him to sleep ever since they'd spilled the truth to Rob seemed like a bed of jagged rock tonight. Gray tossed and turned and tossed some more. Old memories of the last time he'd left Cassie eleven years ago flitted through his mind. Cassie, soft and silken and lying in his arms during those last few earth-shattering minutes, rising up to wrap her arms around his neck, her beautiful breasts brushing his chest, her lips fitted perfectly to his own. She'd kissed him as she refused to let him walk her home. He'd watched her slip away, her hair falling loose around her hips as she left him.

Gray pushed at his pillow as he remembered what came next. Cassie refusing his calls, letting him know that one night had been more than enough for her.

He didn't deny that a part of him had been relieved at the time. He'd known all too well even then the risk of getting too close to any one woman. His mother had walked, his aunt had run, and there had been the young woman his first weeks in college who had asked for his love and then changed her mind. So Gray had known by the time Cassie came along that he didn't want real involvement. Still, he would have liked to have had just a little more time with her back then. And he'd definitely like a few more days now. He didn't want this to be the end just yet.

"Stop it, Alexander," he told himself, sitting up with the sheet wrapped around his hips. "It's been hell these last two days and you know it."

And it had been. Knowing she was in the shower, brushing past her in the small confines of these rooms, struggling to keep his hands off her, watching her smile and wanting to be the one to make her laugh. It was a good thing he was going tomorrow, after all. He should be glad, relieved to have everything over and done.

But two hours later, when he heard Cass's soft murmurs mingling with Rob's, as he listened to her opening and closing drawers and packing her son's things, Gray threw back the covers and pulled on his pants.

He made his way to Rob's room without pausing to allow himself time to think.

"Come with us, Cass," he said simply. "I want you to see where Rob will be staying. This will be his first time with me. You should be there. Just this time."

"See, Mom. I told you." Rob turned those pleading, deep blue eyes on his mother.

Cassie looked down at her son and lightly brushed his hair, grateful for the fact that he was still young enough to want her around. "This is your time with Gray and his father, Rob, and I really have to stay here and work."

"Cass." She couldn't help looking up at Gray when he spoke. His low drawl drew her like no other, but still she shook her head at the admonition in his tone.

"It's not a good idea," she insisted.

It wasn't. This was Rob's first meeting with Hugh and she didn't know what to expect, given the circumstances. Maybe nothing, but she didn't want to do anything that would put her son at a disadvantage. If he showed up alone, there was a chance the man would focus on Rob and not on his unfavorable memories of her or her father. As he should. She didn't want Rob damaged by her past any more than he had been already. For that reason, she planned to give Hugh Alexander a wide berth.

But Gray and Rob apparently had other plans. She saw the silent look they exchanged and Gray's nod as Rob made some quick excuse and left the room.

"Well, that was very smoothly done," she said, trying for a small smile. "Is this your cue to get out the instruments of torture?"

Gray held out his empty hands. "No chains, no feathers to tickle you with until you capitulate. Just you and me talking."

He framed her face with his hands so that she was staring up into his eyes. She let her lashes drift shut, then opened them quickly, backing away.

"You're a fair man," she whispered. "And it's not fair trying to overwhelm my senses when we're talking about something this serious."

"I thought it was my own senses that were being overwhelmed." His slight smile was gentle. He studied her with eyes that were both fierce and tender until she felt he'd actually touched her, though she was now a good three feet away.

The silence grew between them, then he swore beneath his breath. "Come with us, Cass. We want you there."

She moved close and grasped his hands in spite of her resolve to keep some distance. "Don't ask. This is...too difficult."

"I'm sorry. I am, but you're so much a part of this, and I want you there for his first time with me."

"You think I don't want to be there for him?"

"If you do, then come. I'm sure going back into a town where your last memories were humiliating ones won't be easy, but I'll do my best to protect you from all that. Come with us. With my father ill, there may be times when I have to deal with circumstances a child shouldn't be exposed to, and I certainly wouldn't want to leave Rob alone in a strange place."

She hadn't thought of that. What if things didn't go well? What if Hugh were dying? How could she ask Gray to handle his grief and a ten-year-old child at the same time?

Cassie looked up at Gray. She knew he wouldn't force her to come, that he would protect Rob from any harm or frightening elements, and that he would do so at a cost to himself.

She sighed, facing the inevitable. "You're right. I wasn't thinking of that. I'll...of course I'll come."

Gray let out a breath, tightening his grip on her slightly. "Thank you, sweet lady."

His thumbs brushed her wrists, comforting her, even though she knew he must be worried sick about his father.

Her time with Gray had been extended. Because Rob needed her. Because she wanted to help Gray through this rough time. And, all right, darn it, yes, she had agreed in part just because she wanted to be near him for a few days longer.

Blinking hard as if to clear her mind of that errant thought, Cass took a deep breath.

"I'll want to stay in the background, Gray, to just be there for when you and Rob need me. I'll get someone to help here for the few days I'll be gone."

He stepped closer, tucked one finger beneath her chin and tilted her face up to his.

"It won't be so bad. I'll help you through," he whispered, dropping a quick kiss on her forehead. But it wasn't fears for herself, but for Gray, that assailed Cassie as she went back to her room to pack. What would actually happen when they got back to town?

It was one thing for him to bring Rob home, claiming him as his child this time. It was the decent kind of thing people expected of a man like Gray, but to openly acknowledge the mother of that child, as well, to bring her along?

He was Misunderstood's prince, and people expected a great deal of him. They held him to a higher standard, as they always had. She hoped no one would get the wrong idea and think he was planning to marry her just because she was with him. She hoped no one would criticize him when it didn't happen.

Gray tried to look at the town through Cassie's eyes as he slowly drove through the small downtown area heading for the historic section where he was taking her and Rob. The hardware store had been on the outskirts; it was a newer building that hadn't been there eleven years ago. But this—she would remember all of this.

A small sound at his side drew his attention and he turned to see Cass sitting up straighter, staring at buildings she hadn't seen in eleven years.

"It's so much the same, and so very different," she whispered sheepishly when she noticed him watching her.

"Tell me. What's changed, and what do you remember?"

"Oh, I don't know." She held out one hand toward an old brick building. "The beauty shop still looks the same way it did when I first moved here seventeen years ago, but this coffee shop wasn't here, and that building over there…"

Her voice trailed off as she noticed the name above the door.

"It's your office. Of course that wasn't here when I lived here. Did you—do you need to stop in?"

"I will. Later. But thank you." He reached over and took her hand, knowing she had asked for his sake, not her own.

"Are we going to your house, Gray? Is that it over there?"

Gray glanced in his rearview mirror to see Rob tugging on his seat belt as he looked out the car left and right.

"No, Rob," Cassie said. "Gray lives on the edge of town in a huge, white house that looks like something out of a fairy tale when the sun hits it first thing in the morning. He'll show you later, maybe."

"Definitely," Gray concurred. "I'm not there much anymore, since I have my own place in town now, but I'll have to look again. I never quite thought of it in that way." He glanced at Cass who was turning a lovely shade of pink.

"Well, I guess I did have a tendency to romanticize things when I was a girl," she said, shrugging and looking out her window so that all Gray was left with was a view of her profile. Thick lashes, a straight little nose, a determined chin, and that long, lovely neck bisected by the satin of her braid. She hadn't romanticized things for a long time, he would guess. Probably stopped doing that very thing when she found herself with the very real challenge of being pregnant and alone.

"It was just a house when I was a kid," he confessed. "Sometimes too big for my father and myself, but I confess that you make me curious. Morning's first light? Maybe you could show it to me."

She shook her head, fiddling with the buttons that ran down the front of her skirt. "I think you should just look at it with Rob, all right?"

She was right. No good going back.

"You're going to like the place you and your mom are

staying for the next few days," he promised his son, turning down the street toward Tess's house. "It belongs to a friend of mine who just eloped with a really great guy a couple of days ago, so she's moved out of her house. She and her husband are living across the street now. Maybe you've heard of him. I think his name is Jake."

"Jake? Are you kidding? When he called to tell us he was getting married the other day, I didn't think I'd get to see him real soon."

Gray ignored the twinge he felt, witnessing his son's enthusiasm for a man who might have been his father. Rob had known Jake for years while he had only been around for two weeks. Of course it would take time to build a relationship.

"Well, I'm sure he'll stop by to say hi, but I don't know if he'll be around much the next few days," Gray confessed.

"How come? Has he gone somewhere? There's his motorcycle," Rob said as they pulled up in front of Tess's house and climbed out of the car.

Rob was right. The Harley sat in front of the old house across the street, larger than life. Tess's car was there, too, but there were no other signs of life outside the house that was being renovated. Just an open window on the second floor. Clearly a bedroom window.

Gray looked at Cass as if to ask for help.

"You'll do fine," she said, smiling up at him. "I'll just hang around here for moral support in case you need me."

"Well," Gray began. "I don't exactly think Jake is actually out of town, but...well, he's married now. Starting a family. A wife...needs attention."

Rob's brow furrowed. "Like how you told me Mom is always there for me?"

Gray felt pride flood him, and it was all he could do to keep from hugging his son close. Too soon. Way too soon.

"Like that. But don't worry," Gray said. "When I

talked to Tess, she told me that Jake was dying to go fishing.''

Rob fingered the lock on the car. ''That's what he said when he talked to me, too.'' He frowned slightly, then looked up at his father. ''Do you think he'll want to bring his wife along?''

Gray shrugged. ''Probably. But maybe you can help him teach Tess how to bait a hook. Besides, you wouldn't want to appear ungrateful. The lady is lending her house out. I think you're going to like it, too. It's old, and that means lots of great places to hide away. And there's a butterfly garden and a big hammock in the yard you can sleep on if it's warm.''

Rob's smile was automatic. ''Can I look?''

''Look away. Why don't you carry your bag inside and get set up?''

But when Rob had run off and he turned to Cassie to lead her to the door, she put her hand on his arm to stop him.

''Gray, are you really all right with this? This is Tess's house. You were engaged, and even though Tess and I met that day she came to ask me to help her by telling her about Jake, it was only once, and—'' She held out her hands. ''I just thought we'd be staying in a hotel. I'll only be here for a few days, and—''

''And I'm not letting you stay in that excuse for a hotel sitting out on the highway growing weeds between the parking spaces. Tess and I already discussed this. She and I were friends, Cass. It was to be a marriage of convenience, so I'm not grieving, and yes, I want you here. As for Tess, she really liked you that day you met, and she wants you here.''

''I liked her, too,'' Cassie admitted. ''But I never thought I'd be staying in her house.''

Neither had he, but he couldn't take her to his own home. This was Misunderstood, where she had been gossiped about. He wouldn't have anything ugly touching her stay here.

Turning toward the house, Gray placed his hand on the small of her back and led her up the stairs. Her back was warm, but rigid. Her braid brushed his hand with every step. Soft, sweet-smelling stuff, he remembered, and he had a strong desire to stop, loosen her hair, kiss her until that tight look on her face disappeared, and carry her inside.

But his thought was interrupted by the sudden sound of low male laughter carried across the street, followed by a woman's answering laugh.

Cassie missed a step.

Gray caught her around the waist and pulled her in close to him.

"Gray," she said, looking up into his face with great, worried blue eyes. "You're sure this is a good idea? I don't want you to feel—"

"Cass," he whispered, "don't worry. I've known passion in my life. One night in particular stands out in my mind, but that isn't what Tess and I shared. I want you here. You're uncomfortable in Misunderstood and this part of town is out of the way of any curiosity seekers."

"But it's not very convenient for you. Your father's home is on the other side of town."

"Cass."

"Yes?"

"Would you just let me do this? Would you just once stop taking the weight of the world on your shoulders?"

As if to emphasize his words, he cupped his palms around her narrow shoulders, rubbed small circles and realized just how tense she really was.

She leaned her head back, breathed in a deep breath that brought her breasts a bit closer. "You're right. I'm probably making way too big a deal out of this. Do you want to come inside now?"

Another low female giggle drifted across the street.

And Gray knew that if he came even one inch nearer to her, they were both going to be in trouble.

"Gray?"

"Yes. Oh, yes, sweet lady, I'd like to come inside, but I'm not going to. I'm going to leave you here now before I get us both in trouble again."

"Oh."

"Yes. Oh."

"Gray, you don't have to take the whole weight of the world on your shoulders, either. Especially not about the night Rob was conceived. You didn't force me. It takes two to make love."

He closed his eyes, rested his forehead on hers. "And if I wanted to make love to you here, today, are you telling me you'd stop me? I wish you'd tell me that, Cass. It would make this so much easier."

Her silence was so complete he almost would have thought she'd disappeared if he wasn't still touching her. Opening his eyes, pulling back, he stared down at her.

"Would you stop me if I touched you?"

"I hope so, but…I don't know."

He raised his lips in a grimace. "Then I'd better not come inside, because standing here this close makes me want to move closer."

She studied his expression and then lightly touched his face. "You need to be close to someone because you're worried. You'll be going to see your father now."

"Yes, the nurse said he'd be done with his tests by noon. It's nearly that now."

"Take as long as you need. When things are better, you and Rob can spend some time together."

But no word about her. Nothing about her part in all this, so Gray knew she had meant what she said. She was here just for Rob and himself. This town held no good memories for her. The night he treasured most had only brought her pain.

Hastily he scribbled a number down on a slip of paper and tucked it into her palm.

"I'll be back tonight. Call if you need anything." But he knew she wouldn't call. She was perfectly capable, and she really didn't need him at all.

That was good because she was a woman alone and according to her, she would always be a woman alone. He should be glad she was so damned capable. As a leader in the town, people were always relying on him to help solve their problems. He should be relieved that this woman didn't want or need his help at all.

So why did he still feel this overwhelming need to protect her? And why did he feel guilty dragging her into this town where she hadn't wanted to come?

A scant ten hours later, he knew the reason why. His father had been pale and groggy, but he was also adamant that he would expect a full accounting in the next few days about what Gray had been up to, running off and leaving his business just because a mere woman had jilted him.

That hadn't bothered Gray. He'd simply been relieved to hear that with bed rest, proper exercise and the right diet, his father would be fine. But leaving the house, Gray had run smack into Dora Averly, one of his former teachers. A woman who thrived on bad news.

"I heard you drove into town with Cassandra Pratt and her child in your car, Grayson," she said, crossing her arms. "Is that really true?"

Gray felt a moment of irritation. "Cassie and Rob are visiting. Yes."

"Hmm. I wonder why." She looked at him expectantly.

Well, she could just wonder. For now.

"This is her hometown, Dora. She doesn't need a reason to be here."

The woman pursed her lips. She didn't move out of his

way. "Cassandra was one of my students, you know. Smart, too. It was a shame how she turned out, but then, her father always was a complete drunk who probably didn't give her any direction."

"I wouldn't know about that, Dora. I never really knew the man, but I do know that Cass is an admirable woman. I respect her greatly, and she has a right to expect common courtesy in this town. You can tell that to anyone you meet. Now, if you'll excuse me?"

Gray's mind was seething as he drove back toward Cass. Maybe Dora was just one person, but he knew that people like her were the very reason Cass had left town in the first place, the very reason she hadn't wanted to come back. What's more, he knew he couldn't dismiss people like Dora as much as he'd like to. This was Misunderstood and he did have to tread carefully with Cassie, to protect her whether she felt she needed protecting or not.

She'd been hurt in this town, terribly hurt, and he had been a part of it. The fact that he could so easily become a part of hurting her again, just by being too close to her, was obvious. He had to keep some distance and rein in his ever present desire, but the very thought of keeping away from her when he had only this small amount of time remaining chafed. And not just because he wanted her in his bed so badly it made him shake just to think of it.

She was his friend. They shared a child. It was only natural that he would want to be near her.

"Keep dreaming, Alexander. Are you talking forever here?"

Why not? He had once planned on marrying Tess and he and Tess had shared a great deal less than he and Cass did.

What would marriage with Cassie be like?

Probably impossible. She'd told him she wouldn't have a marriage of convenience.

But that had been two weeks ago. And since then they'd

spent time together. She'd grown to like him at least a little, she'd admitted she liked his touch, and she *had* allowed him to bring her son here. Marriage would be a practical solution that would solve a lot of problems.

Surely by now she would see the sense in such a plan if he argued his case well enough.

Chapter Ten

Cassie sat bolt upright in bed and stared at the red digital eleven on the bedside alarm clock.

"Rob?" she whispered when she heard the small sound from beyond her door. Rising, she realized that someone was at the front door. Carefully, she made her way to the door and, leaving the chain on, lifted the latch.

"It's only me," Gray whispered, and she quickly let him inside. "I would have called, but I didn't want to wake Rob."

"Gray, what—"

"Shh, Cass." She felt the heat of his body as Gray closed the door behind him and leaned closer to her. "I'm sorry I woke you, sweetheart, but I've been thinking all night. You and I—we need to talk."

Oh no. That serious tone in his voice, that sound—

"Is it your father? Is he worse?"

In the dark she bumped against him, and he slid his palms up her arms, steadying her. "No, no, nothing like that. It's just that being here, realizing how things are, Cass, I think we should consider marriage again. I do."

She blinked, still not sure she wasn't dreaming this whole scene in the first place. Gray here in the dark, holding her, touching her, asking her to marry him. It was what she'd once dreamed of every night and now here she was back in the same town where she had experienced all those dreams.

"No." She blinked rapidly, trying to clear the fog from her eyes.

"Yes. Please." He pulled her closer, molded his body to hers. Clad only in a thin cotton nightshirt, she could feel the heat of him as he held her. She didn't need the light to know his lips were just a touch away from her own.

"Gray, you're not thinking. It's late, and you're tired."

That was all it was, because she couldn't allow herself to think he was really serious. She had noticed things today that he probably hadn't seen. Even just driving through town, people had stopped to look at him, admiration and welcome in their eyes. He was the heart of this town. And she?

Well, she hadn't missed seeing the few people who recognized her, either. Those who glanced from her to her son and then quickly looked away, as if promiscuity were contagious. Gray hadn't seen. He would have tried to protect her if he'd noticed, but it was the way things were.

She looked up, opening her mouth to speak, but he gathered her close. "Marry me, Cass," he said, whispering his lips across her own. She closed her eyes. Here in the dark it was so easy to believe that the world wasn't real, that it was just her and Gray, and Gray's family and his place in this town didn't matter. It was so tempting to pretend he loved her.

She found his chest with her fingertips, walked her hands up around his neck by feel alone, slanted her head to meet his kiss. His mouth was firm, warm, and demanding as he pulled her closer and her breasts met his chest.

If she were only foolish enough to make believe she didn't know what the consequences of giving in to this need were, she could have him. For just tonight she could have him once more. A whole night of touching Gray and of Gray touching her back.

"Marry me," he urged again.

His words were a wakeup call. Something had happened or he wouldn't be asking. She wanted nothing more than to tell herself that wasn't so, to take him to her bed and lie with him all night. But what she wanted was immaterial.

For two seconds, maybe three, she took his kisses and gave back her own, allowing herself to savor the feel of his heated skin beneath her fingers. Then, pulling away, she kept her hands firmly on his chest. An arm's-length distance wasn't much, but it would have to be enough.

"We can't do this, Gray, and we can't marry. We made a mistake once before. Let's not make two."

"Yes, we could marry," he argued, reaching out for her, but she held her arms firm.

"Why? Give me reasons." She hoped he couldn't hear the pleading in her voice. She wanted him to convince her, she thought, horrified at herself. It would take so little, just one little word.

"Cass," he drawled. "We share a son." His words fell into the night. Simple. Undeniable. He was into his rational businessman mode now, and she knew he wanted to win this argument. He had won so many arguments in his life. Why not this one? His reason sounded so...well, reasonable. To him, she was sure it was exactly that.

"Yes. We do." She wanted to give him a smile in the darkness, but somehow couldn't manage to keep her lips from trembling. "But I knew that already."

"You want more? You need reasons? Then I'll give you reasons, sweet Cass. I respect you, and I always will. I want to provide for you and Rob. That's not such a terrible thing, is it?''

''It's a wonderful thing,'' she agreed. ''I respect you, too.''

''Then marry me, sweetheart. You know we'd be good together…that we're friends, that I desire you.'' And framing her with his hands, he swept his fingers up her body, along her thighs, smoothing over her hips, grazing the tips of her breasts, caressing her throat and her lips, then gently closing her eyelids with his fingertips. He didn't try to still the tremble that made his hand shake as he touched her. ''You do this to me every time,'' he said. ''Even just thinking of touching you, I shake.''

''And you know that I shiver at your touch, too,'' she told him, rising on her toes, leaning forward to press one soft kiss on his lips. ''I want you, Gray. Too much. But I—I can't marry you.''

He opened his mouth to protest, and she laid her fingers over his lips.

''Gray, we can't marry. We just…don't fit. Your place is here. You're a prince in this town, you know. I always thought of you that way, and it's true. People look up to you, because you're kind and caring and just. They count on you for so many things. And I don't belong here,'' she said, releasing him from the gentle cage of her fingers. ''We've discussed this before, and besides, you were engaged to another woman just two weeks ago. There would be talk.''

He stroked her hair back from her forehead, cupped her face in his hands and kissed her. ''I wouldn't hurt you for the world,'' he promised. ''I would never, ever, want to hurt you again. But you're right. We've had this talk before. It's getting repetitive. I won't bore you by asking again.''

And slipping from her side, he left her. The door clicked softly as he locked himself out.

Only then did she place both hands over her mouth to keep herself from crying out. Gray wanted her. Gray had always wanted her, and she had always wanted him. He respected her and wanted to protect her and Rob. If only she could be a different kind of woman. If only she could just marry and not care about love.

But it was impossible. She would just have to learn how to live with this arrangement. Gray was Rob's father, and he would be a good father. Close to his child. She was glad for that. But soon, very soon, there would be no "Gray and Cassie and Rob," only "Gray and Rob" or "Cassie and Rob." She and Gray would always be apart and after she was sure Rob had made himself comfortable here, she would never allow herself to return. She would not seek Gray out or let him seek her out anymore. The sooner the transition was made, the sooner she could end this pain and longing.

So what about tomorrow? She'd been having nightmares for days. And now she was here and Hugh's illness was a reality. Gray had not said much, but he must have been worried. He had seemed so lost. If Hugh was really ill, how would he react to the shock of meeting a half-grown grandson he never wanted? Someone might be hurt. The chances were very good that someone would be hurt. She couldn't hold her silence any longer.

The moon was beginning to fade, but Gray had been lying in bed for hours, not even pretending to sleep.

He could still feel Cass on his fingertips, hear her voice shivering through his body, call up the taste of her without even trying.

She'd called him the prince of the town, and for once he cursed his privileged status, because she had never been made to feel like a princess, and now he would never get to treat her that way.

She'd be gone soon. He was losing her again. Soon the

two of them would only talk in those rare moments when they bundled Rob back and forth. He and Cass would live separate lives. They would communicate only on the surface.

And wasn't that what he'd always wanted? he thought, readjusting his pillow one more time. An orderly life, uncluttered by the emotional baggage others carried around?

Yes, and maybe he would have that again if he could just get beyond this...unreasonable ache. Once Cass was gone, he would surely adjust. And so, rolling over, Gray concentrated on exorcising the lady from his thoughts.

But hours later she was still on his mind. Only because she'd called him on the phone at dawn asking for directions to his place, he reasoned. Because he was looking down at her as she stood in the doorway, pale and morning beautiful, nervously pleating the hem of her blouse with her fingers.

"I'm sorry if I woke you," she whispered, "but we have to talk. It's about Rob. I'm not sure you should be introducing him to your father today."

He leaned on the door frame, trying to get his moorings, to figure out what had happened to bring that look to her face.

"I'm sure it's difficult sharing him when you've had him to yourself for such a long time," he said slowly, a bit too carefully. "But it's time, Cass. You know that."

She bit down on her lip and shook her head. "That's not it. It's not just the sharing. It's that...maybe springing a grandson on your father when he's not well isn't wise."

Gray smiled. He rested one hand on the wall above her head and looked down at her. "Sooner or later he's going to figure it out on his own. He's not a stupid man, Cass."

She jerked her head up. "I know."

"He's bound to hear something anytime now. The town thought Jake was Rob's father until Tess told them it wasn't true. Now I've shown up with you and Rob. It's not going to take long for people to figure it out."

Closing her eyes, she leaned back against the wall. "And how do you think he's going to react to all of this? I don't want Rob hurt. What if your father is upset?"

Gray slid one finger beneath her chin, urging her to open her eyes and look at him.

"He'll be overjoyed to have a grandson," he assured her.

Slowly she shook her head. "I know you think that, Gray, but I'm not so sure. Rob's my son, and your father and I...well, the fact that Rob is mine could make a difference to the man. He may want a grandson, but maybe...not this one."

"Cass, what are you talking about?"

She dropped her gaze from his and crossed her arms over her chest. "I know your father isn't a stupid man, because I lived in this town, but that's not the only reason. The day after you and I—made Rob, your father came to see me. He must have suspected something was happening between us."

"You never told me you'd talked to him."

She shook her head, her braid jerking with the movement.

"I couldn't. I was scared and ashamed and unsure of what to do. He told me he didn't want me hanging around his son and that he didn't want you to have anything to do with a Pratt. He promised he'd take what little my family had if I saw you again. I guess he thought—" She stuffed her hands into her pockets defiantly, turning her face away from his. "I think perhaps he thought there was something more between you and I than there really was, that I might be in love with you."

Her words were low, but fierce.

"But you didn't love me."

"No, I didn't." Her voice rose and stiffened in denial.

Gray felt a tightening in his chest at her words. Wounded pride, he told himself. She hadn't loved him, but then he didn't believe in love, either, did he? Of course he didn't. He never had.

And it was unimportant what he believed in or felt at this moment, he realized, watching her. She removed her hands from her pockets and clenched her arms tightly around herself, as if to keep from crumbling. He wondered what that kind of humiliation must feel like, to have someone reduce you to nothingness, a human being with no worth. She, who went out of her way to make a faltering old man feel young and dignified and valued. A woman who worried about the comfort of a man who had stolen her virginity, with no thought to what that might mean to her. A mother who had sacrificed all she had for her child had been made to feel like a pariah in the town she had grown up in...because her family had been poor, because her parents had been uneducated, because her father had been a drunk that no one wanted to deal with. Everyone had made her feel that she was different because of that, including himself, but his father had put it into cutting, cruel words when he'd told her his son was too good for a Pratt. She had been faulted for her father's mistakes when she was so young and vulnerable.

"You should have told me."

"I—I almost did. Once I even went to your college to talk to you, but I...went back home without saying anything."

A spark of anger rose within Gray, but not at Cass. Of course she hadn't told him. What would she have said? After his own careless use of her and his father's visit, she'd probably had more than her fill of Alexanders. And now she was being forced to deal with them again.

"I'm sorry, sweetheart," he said. "More sorry than I can tell you."

He fought against the urge to take her in his arms, whisper his sorrow to her. He and his had caused her so much pain. She deserved so much more. She deserved to be left alone.

Purposefully he turned toward the door.

"Where are you going?"

"To see my father, of course. He hurt you, Cass. A man who preached responsibility to me all my life, and yet he apparently thought nothing of harming a young, innocent girl."

She was shaking her head frantically. "I wasn't innocent, Gray."

He stared her straight in the eye. "Yes. You were. Even though I'd touched you. And even if you hadn't been, he had no right to talk to you that way. The man owes you. An apology, at the very least."

Her eyes widened. She sucked in a deep, frantic breath. "Please don't. I don't want anything from him."

But of course, she wanted nothing to do with the Alexanders anymore. That was why she had run, why she had been in hiding for eleven years. And he himself had brought them back into her life.

Taking a deep breath, he lifted one hand to her, then let it drop to his side. "I want to make amends in some way."

"No. Don't feel that way. There's no need. I'm not seventeen anymore. I've lived past it. But...don't confront your father. You and I have already made too many mistakes. I don't want to upset a sick man. And...if he's going to meet Rob, is it really a good idea to bring up the past?"

"Rob is a part of the past."

"To us, but to your father and to Rob, it's the first time they'll really be meeting. They know nothing of each other. What do you think your father will think of him?"

Gray couldn't help it then. He took her by the arms, looked down into her anxious eyes.

"How could anyone not warm to him instantly, Cass?" But he knew what she was saying was true, because how could anyone look into this lady's eyes and say hurtful things to her? And yet his father had done just that.

She locked her gaze with his, leaning closer, as if her nearness could convince him to see things her way. "Ordinarily I think anyone would like Rob, but then, I'm his mother. And if your father knows about me...if he remembers, and you throw me in his face, he might be defensive and angry."

"He doesn't deserve to meet Rob."

Gray couldn't help thinking that way. If Hugh had come to see Cassie just a day earlier, there would be no Rob. She never would have made love with him. Her pride was too great. The pain would have stopped her.

And it was her pain right now that was stopping *him,* he conceded.

"All right, I won't confront him on this, but only because I don't want him hurting you or Rob again. I promise I won't, Cass," he said when that slightly anxious look still lingered in her gaze.

"Thank you, Gray. I'm sorry I didn't tell you all of this earlier, but—thank you."

She smiled up at him. The warmth and brightness came back into her eyes, and his Cass was back.

His Cass. He wondered when he'd started thinking of her that way. His Cass. His.

He leaned close and looped one arm around her waist, pulling her to him for one quick, hard kiss.

"To seal the bargain, so you'll know I'll keep my promise," he told her.

"As if I thought otherwise. Haven't I told you before that I know you're a man of your word, Gray?"

But it wasn't enough to be a man of his word anymore. He was an Alexander, something he'd always been proud of and now regretted. For he and his had hurt this woman and had stolen a piece of her pride. How she must hate all the Alexanders. No wonder she had no desire to become his wife.

The pain squeezed tighter, and he knew that he wanted her for reasons more complex than the ones he had told her. But he couldn't think about that now. He had promised her it was a closed subject, and she would count on him to stand by that.

"Gray, what about Rob and your father? She was leaning back against his arm, a question in her eyes.

He let out a deep breath. "I don't know. I don't feel he deserves to meet Rob now, but—"

"But what would you tell Rob?" She gently supplied the end of the sentence he had begun.

"Yes. I brought him here to meet his grandfather. I don't want him to think that I'm ashamed to be his father. To cancel this meeting now might imply that."

She nodded solemnly. "Then I suppose we'd better wake him up."

"I'll take good care of him. I'll protect him."

"I trust you, Gray."

As she had never trusted him in the past, he realized.

With her secrets or her son. But then she had no choice this time, did she? Once again the Alexanders had forced her hand.

And this time, Gray swore, he wouldn't fail her.

"It feels strange not to have Mom coming with us."

Gray stared across the passenger seat right into his son's blue eyes. Cassie's eyes. Worried eyes, he thought. All wrong for a child, he thought, struggling for the words that would banish the worry.

"She wanted you to have some time alone with your grandfather and me." It wasn't a complete lie. Cassie was considerate of others' feelings. She would have wanted her son to have a chance to get to know his grandfather even if there hadn't been that other problem. He had no doubt that it was so.

"Will I be staying here sometime? Mom says I probably will."

Gray pulled the car over to the side. He turned to Rob.

"I hope so, Rob. I know this can't be easy for you. Having a father and a grandfather and a new town to get used to. But I hope—I really hoped you'll want to stay with me now and then. That you'll give me a chance to be a real father to you."

Rob fiddled with the door lock. "It's just been Mom and me so far. I never thought about grandparents. Mom's are dead, you know. Does yours—your dad, know about me?"

"Yes." He'd called him just that morning to break the news, but Hugh, as he'd suspected, had already heard hints of rumors and had demanded that they come immediately.

A low whoosh of air seeped out of Rob and he sat back in the seat quietly. "Good. I don't like surprises all that much. Not that kind."

Gray knew just what Rob meant. Reaching out, he smoothed one hand over his son's hair, risked his first touch. "Everything will be fine, son," he promised, praying he was right. And if he wasn't? Well, he defied his father and anyone else in the world to say one harmful thing to this child. No bonds of blood or past history would stop him from protecting Rob from any insult or injury.

But as it turned out, that wasn't necessary.

"Fine-looking young man," Hugh Alexander said, taking his glasses off the side table. "Come closer and tell me about yourself, son," the old man said. "Do you like this sweet little town of mine? Would you like to come here and stay?"

Rob watched the man with serious eyes as he neared the bed. "It's a pretty nice town. I'd like to visit, I think."

Hugh's laugh was deep and bellowing. "A diplomat.

Mark of an Alexander. I like that. I do." And he proceeded to quiz his grandson on his hobbies and grades in school.

"Why don't you run off now and see if my cook can't scrounge up some cookies for you? Won't let me have any lately, but I'll bet she's got some squirreled away," he confided after he and Rob had been talking for a few minutes. "Your father and I will have a talk and get caught up on business while you do that."

And in a few minutes, Gray found himself alone with the man he was seeing with new eyes.

"You've got yourself a fine son there," Hugh said. "But it's no good a boy like that living without his father all those years."

Gray couldn't agree more, but opening that topic could lead to others. Things he'd promised Cass he wouldn't discuss.

"His mother's a wonderful woman. She raised him well. And singlehandedly, too," he said simply.

The other man nodded. "But you're going to marry her now. Now that you know. I assume you didn't know before, because I didn't raise you to shirk your responsibilities."

"He's not just someone's responsibility." Even as he said the words, Gray seemed to remember Cass herself saying something quite like that just two weeks ago.

"Never said that. I said you should marry the mother. Won't have anything less. I don't want to see my grandson growing up a bastard."

It occurred to Gray that his father hadn't wanted a great many things. He hadn't really wanted to take the time away from his business for his family. He hadn't wanted his son to waste his time on too many friendships when he could be learning the business. He hadn't wanted Cassie anywhere near his son just because her father had problems and her family had no money. And now he didn't want his grandson growing up a bastard. The fact that he had even used the word in reference to Rob made Gray want to slam his fist into a wall.

"Well, are you going to marry the woman?"

"The woman." As if Cassie were just a game piece to be moved around the board.

Gray shifted his position. He concentrated on keeping his body relaxed and on remembering he had promised Cass he wouldn't bring up the past.

"There's nothing I want more than to marry Rob's mother," Gray said quietly. "Nothing. Unfortunately, she doesn't want me, and it seems she has an aversion to the Alexander name."

Hugh's eyes were like cold obsidian when he looked at his son. "What's wrong with the woman, son? Has she no sense? No decency? Is she out of her mind?"

The insult to Cassie hit home, and Gray fought his rage at knowing Cass had stood before this man and been shamed when she was still too young to fight for herself.

"Don't say any more," he warned. "You're talking about a woman I respect and revere."

A woman I love beyond belief.

The words just slipped in. He didn't know where they'd come from, but he knew they were truth as soon as the thought formed. *I love Cassandra Pratt* rolled through his mind as he nodded to his father, excused himself and drove away with Rob.

Love. The very thing he'd run from all his life. Because he didn't want to risk losing the one he loved. And yet he'd fallen in love with Cass. Deeply. Hopelessly. And he wouldn't have it any other way, even though he'd lost her without ever having won her.

He'd asked her to marry him, and she'd said no. And not just because she didn't want to marry, but because she didn't want to marry him specifically. She'd told him he was the town prince, but the Pratts had been treated by some, by his father, as peasants. The Alexanders had made

Cass's life in this town unbearable. His child in her belly was the reason she'd gotten expelled and fled her home.

She hadn't wanted him invading her world again.

And that was the problem with love, the catch he'd known was there all along. Because he loved Cass, he would give her her heart's desire. He'd get out of her life as much as he could, and damn whatever his own desire might be.

Chapter Eleven

"I'm sure everything is going fine, Cass." Tess Walker's voice broke into her thoughts and Cass gazed around the nearly empty restaurant where she and Tess and Jake were sitting. She realized she had been paying no attention at all to her new friend, and Cass felt a moment of guilt. But right now, concern for Rob and Gray filled her mind completely.

"I'm sorry. Was I being totally rude?" she asked, glancing up from her cold cup of coffee. Jake and Tess had arrived an hour ago. They'd taken her under their wing and brought her to lunch at the Silver Platter Diner.

"No such thing," Tess said. "You're just doing what any mother does ninety percent of her time. Worrying."

Cass looked into the other woman's eyes. "I am. But I'm still sorry for my poor manners. Especially since you and Jake are working so hard to cheer me up and take my mind off things. And on your honeymoon, too."

"Hey, Cass, that's what best buddies are for," he reminded her. "You've done your share of cheering me up over the years. Besides, Tess and I need you to make us look respectable for an afternoon. Everyone knows we've been holed up in our house together ever since we got married. The woman just doesn't want to leave the—"

"Jake!" Tess's cheeks were bright pink as she gently punched him on the arm.

"I was just going to say that you didn't want to leave the reconstruction of our house to strangers." He smiled at his wife, dropping a kiss on her nose. Then, rising to pay the check, he led the two women toward the door, pausing to introduce Cassie to the Reverend Matt Harper, a man with a warm smile who hadn't been here eleven years ago. Matt was sitting next to Craig Bickerson, who owned the drugstore, and told Cass she was just as pretty as ever.

Jake looked her way when they had passed beyond the two men and out the door. "Admit it. Misunderstood isn't quite the way you remember it, is it? There are good people here."

Cass tilted her head. "Are you trying to make a point?"

Jake smiled and took his wife's hand. "Maybe, but we can talk about that later. For now I'm trying to get you home. I just saw Gray and Rob drive past on one of the cross streets."

Instant panic took over Cass's body. She barely registered Jake leading the way to the car or the ride back to the house. But when she walked through the door, followed by Jake and Tess, her sight returned full force. She looked at Rob and saw that he seemed unfazed. She turned to Gray, and the rest of the room disappeared.

She wasn't sure what she had expected to happen. Maybe that he and Rob would disappear into Hugh Alexander's house and never return, or that he would return from his father's home and look at her with new and more critical eyes.

And he *was* looking at her differently, studying her as

though he'd never seen her before. As if he wanted something from her. As if he had something to tell her.

"Cass," was all he said, but his tone was gentle.

"Is everything...all right?" With Rob in the room, he couldn't say much, but she needed some reassurance anyway.

"Hey, Rob," she heard Tess say gently, "Jake and I are going to go pound some nails. Want to come?"

Cass felt her son's eyes on her as he looked between her and Gray. Rob had become more suspicious in the past few days.

His innocence had been chipped away a bit, but he smiled at Tess. "Sure, what are we going to fix? You want to come, too...Gray? He's really good with a hammer," Rob explained, looking to his father.

"Wouldn't miss it," Gray said. "Just let me have a few words with your mother, all right?"

So Tess and Jake and Rob were already heading out when the bell rang. Tess opened the door.

"A message for Cassandra Pratt," the man said, looking straight into Gray's eyes.

Tess took the envelope, passed it to Cass, and with a meaningful look at Gray, herded everyone else outside.

Cass stared down at the white vellum where her name was scrolled in black. She looked at Gray, a question in her eyes.

"My father's driver," he said quietly. "I can leave the room if you'd like some privacy."

"No." She didn't know what was in that note and she probably should have asked to be alone, but she knew that whatever was there, she would share with him. Besides, her fingers were like fumbling icicles, and Gray was...warmth.

And so he was there when she ripped the envelope open and when she read the brief message and held it out to him.

"He's asked me to come see him."

He took the piece of paper from her, raised one brow. "Asked, Cass?"

His tone actually drew a small smile from her. "All right, he says that he's heard a rumor that I'm the mother of his grandchild, and yes, it's a summons, not a request. Of course, there's no need for your father and I to meet."

Gray admired the firm tilt of her chin, but he hadn't missed the tremors that had preceded her efforts to control herself. He took her hand into his own, brushed his thumb across her palm. "I think you should go."

"Why?"

He breathed in deeply, studying her for long seconds. "You're a strong woman, Cass, one of the strongest I know. But my father once threatened and hurt you, and you're still dealing with that incident. I think you need to face him in order to put the past to rest." And maybe if she could do that, if she could recover from that wound a bit, someday she might look at this man who loved her and learn to care for him, just a little.

"Not necessary," she insisted. "The past is...just history."

"So, you don't want to go."

"I don't *need* to go."

Her words were firm, but her eyes weren't focused on him as directly as they should have been. Gray hated that. He wanted her looking at him with conviction and no fear.

"And what if I told you my father ordered us to marry a scant hour ago because he doesn't want Rob to be a bastard?"

The breath she took was audible. Her fingers clenched on his own. "He didn't say that. Not that about Rob."

"Yes. He did."

She tipped up her chin and studied him. Carefully.

"You think I should see him. Are you trying to manipulate me into going, Gray?"

"Absolutely. No question."

Her hands were cold against his, but she was looking at him now. Dead-on.

"Why?"

"Because I want you to win this time. You're not a young, scared girl anymore. You've moved so far beyond that. I want you to meet him, to talk to him, to assert yourself and gain back some of the self-respect he and I stole from you. If I could do this for you, I would, sweetheart. I would rewrite history."

He brought his hands up to frame her face, stared down into her eyes.

"Everything that happened wasn't bad," she whispered.

"No, it wasn't. I remember one glorious day in particular. The day we made love was very special." And he slipped his hands up through her hair, cupped her head in his palms.

Cass swallowed, parting her lips, then closing them again when he moved nearer. She nodded, loosening herself from his hold.

"All right. Maybe I *should* go. It might be a good thing...to get beyond the memories of the past."

The look on her face, her tone...Gray knew they were talking about two different things. She meant to get beyond her attraction to him, he was sure. But at least she was taking a step. He had at least convinced her of that. It was all he could do for now.

"I'll come with you."

"For strength? To protect me? I know you'd do that, but no. If I'm going to make this work, I have to be able to walk in there on my own two feet and leave the same way. No crutches, no help."

She was right. Of course, she was right. She didn't need him, and had proven that before all too well.

The house was huge, even larger on the inside than it looked on the outside. And imposing. Tons of dark wood, walls that reached to the heavens, floors that clicked and echoed the sound of footsteps.

Cassie followed the stiff-backed servant who led her up a flight of stairs into a room the size of her own house three times over. She couldn't help looking up at the carving on the panels that encased the entire room. A person who wasn't careful to guard against intimidation could easily feel small in such an imposing room.

"Beautiful, isn't it, this place of mine?"

She whirled and faced the man who was sitting in the corner of the room as if he hadn't wanted her to notice he was there.

"It's...lovely, Mr. Alexander," Cass said, forcing coolness into her voice. "But then, I'm sure you know that. You wanted to see me?"

"This house has known generations of Alexanders." He motioned her to a large wing-back chair. "The Alexander name stands for something in this town. Leadership. Integrity. Industriousness. Pride. My son is an Alexander, Ms. Pratt. He used to believe in all those qualities."

"And he still does," she said with a small tilt of her head. "His short association with me hasn't changed that."

His sharp bark of laughter echoed off the walls. "Ah, touched a nerve, did I? You haven't forgotten our meeting then, either?"

"No, not at all."

"But you still slept with my son. Against my wishes."

Cassie held herself very still. He didn't know that Rob had been conceived before that day, not after. She had no intention of letting him know that she had, indeed, followed his orders to the letter.

"Your son is an Alexander, Ms. Pratt."

She took a deep breath. This she had been expecting.

"No. He's not."

"You could marry my son."

"That's not a possibility."

"Because you don't like me. Maybe you don't like Gray so much anymore, either. But think, Ms. Pratt, what you'd have if you married him. You could give your son the Alexander name. You could have all this or something very much like this. Gray has money of his own. You could be rich. A very rich woman."

Cassie took a deep breath, feeling the anger spark to life within her. Hugh Alexander was clearly still as arrogant as ever.

He smiled. "You hadn't considered that before had you? Maybe because you hadn't been here to see just what wealth the Alexanders hold. It could be yours, too, and all you need to do—"

His mouth was still moving but Cassie had ceased to hear his words. What was the point in listening, after all, when there could never be any common ground between her and this man who clearly thought he had the power to manipulate her?

She clenched her hands on the arms of the chair at the very thought. She realized that years ago, she had indeed, let this man call the shots, let him talk her into turning away from the finest man she'd ever known. Even if she and Gray were never destined for forever, the little time they could have had would have been special. But she'd missed all that. Because she'd let *this* man run her life.

But that was then. This was now.

"I'm sure that when you take the time to review the situation, you'll see that marriage to Gray could be beneficial to you. It could change your life." He smiled, and Cass knew that he thought she would come around. He was used to bending people to his will. He had reason to believe she would give in to him. Easily.

He was wrong.

Slowly she lifted one brow. She rose from her chair.

"I'm sorry, but I'm afraid that won't be a possibility, Mr. Alexander. I don't want your money. I'm not at all interested in your offer, and I definitely won't be marrying your son."

His face remained blank for two, maybe three, seconds, as though he didn't quite believe what he was hearing. Then his mouth twisted in anger.

Cass simply stood there looking down at him, her chin held high.

"You'll think about it awhile," he finally said. "You'll change your mind. When your pride has had a chance to heal, you'll see that money can make a difference. It always does when a person really thinks."

"I can guarantee that won't happen this time...Hugh. Not with me."

"Especially with you. You have a great deal to gain."

Cass looked at the man who clearly wanted something from her, who was willing to go so far as to threaten and bribe to get his way, and in that moment, the thoughts that had been gathering for the last few minutes finally gelled. The tumblers clicked into place. She had lived eleven years in fear of this man because she thought that he held the power. But she'd been wrong. He didn't have any power over her, not if she didn't allow him to. Not anymore. Her parents were gone. Hugh had no one to ruin. He couldn't control her life, and she wouldn't allow him to control her son's life, either.

For the first time ever Cassie looked at Hugh Alexander and didn't think of him as larger than life. He was just a man, and not a very nice one.

"I'm sorry, but I have other things to do, Mr. Alexander," she said. "And you and I have nothing more to talk about, after all, do we?"

She turned and walked directly to the door, slowly, her shoulders back, her head high. She heard him call her name, but she didn't stop until she reached the doorway. Then she turned and stared him directly in the eyes.

"You were right about one thing, and only one thing, Mr. Alexander. This *is* a very nice house. And you're welcome to it. All of it."

And then she swept from the room. It wasn't until she made it down the hall, down the stairs, out the big heavy doors and into the car she had borrowed from Gray that her legs turned to jelly and she realized the emotional toll the last few moments had taken on her. She threw the car in gear, drove carefully down the long drive and around the corner. She kept going for at least a mile. And then she stopped. She pulled the car off to the side of the road and sat, reviewing the implications of her visit with Hugh.

The man had offered to bribe her, to buy her, to force a marriage between her and Gray whether either of them wanted this marriage or not.

He didn't even care about his own son's feelings. That much was clear.

And one other thing was clear, as well. She had to leave, to go home. It was past time. Coming to Misunderstood had been a mistake, except...this day, these last few moments, had jolted her out of the fog she'd been living in for a long while. Because the truth was that she had come here for Rob, but it was time to leave because she loved Gray and had wanted to be near him. She loved him with a woman's heart this time. For a short time she'd enjoyed his kisses, his caresses, his desire. She'd loved...just being near him.

But she couldn't have him. Ever. She'd always known that, but now with Hugh's offer staring her in the face, it was time to face reality. Her time with Gray was gone.

She couldn't see him again. She was a horrid liar. He'd dig the truth about his father's insulting bribe out of her in no time. And no matter what she felt about Hugh, the truth was that the man was still Gray's father, still Rob's grandfather.

She'd been dragging out her goodbye, but now it was time for her to return to her world and for Gray to return to his. Soon, very soon, she was sure, he'd begin looking for the kind of woman he really wanted to marry.

And now, at last, the first sharp shards of pain found their way into her heart. She was finally free of the threat of Hugh Alexander, but she wondered if she would ever be free of the longing for his son.

With tears in her throat, Cass put the car in drive and headed for the road home. She had spent long years depending only on herself, and today she had proven to herself that she was indeed, strong. Well, now it was time to be even stronger. It was time again to submerge her feelings. She would do her best to begin learning how not to care, how to stop loving Gray. It was the way things had to be, and would be. Beginning tomorrow.

But for just this one last day, alone with her memories, she would allow herself to open up and love Gray. Completely. For just this day, she would allow herself to cry.

Chapter Twelve

"Do you think she'll be back soon?" Rob was flipping the pages on a book on North American mammals, but his question told Gray that their minds were completely in tune. Cassie hadn't returned yet, and he couldn't imagine what she and his father were finding to talk about. He wished he'd gone with her. He should have gone with her. Even if he'd sat in the car so that she could go in alone and satisfy her need for bravery, he could have offered support of some type.

Gray set aside his still untouched book. He just couldn't concentrate. "She wouldn't stay away too long. Probably ran into someone she used to know when she lived here. I'm sure some of her friends are still in the area."

That seemed to be enough for Rob, but Gray couldn't settle down again. He climbed the stairs to the room where she'd been sleeping and studied the few articles she'd placed on the dresser. A comb for that beautiful long hair, a picture of Rob, a tiny bottle of perfume.

Moving to the dresser he picked it up, taking in a small breath. Lavender. Fresh. Sweet. Like her.

The bed held no trace of her having lain there, but he remembered what she'd felt like the other night, and he realized that memories would soon be all of her he'd ever have. The thought filled him with an ache that stole his breath.

When the phone began ringing in the upstairs study, he hoped it was her and quickly moved to pick it up.

"Gray?"

"Cass, where are you? Are you all right?"

"I'm fine," she said so emphatically that he could almost see her nodding, her braid sliding up and down her shoulder.

"Gray, I—I'm home. I had to come back, to relieve Nancy, who was taking care of the store for me. I realized—it was too much to ask someone to take over my business for more than a couple of days. If you could just get Rob packed, I'll pick him up. Tomorrow. I'll come and get him. All right?"

Oh, God. What had that man said to her, done to her? Maybe he shouldn't have encouraged their meeting, after all. But he was selfish and he'd wanted to make everything right, to turn the clock back so he could have a chance to win her heart. Because he wanted to free her of all the bad that had ever happened to her. And now something had happened. Not something good, either.

"Cassie, talk to me. Don't hang up. Just…talk to me. What happened? Are you home? Are you hurt? Hurting? What happened, love?"

The silence was unbearable. He wanted to crawl right through the wires to get to her, to take her in his arms and hold her until she spilled all her hurt, all her troubles. Until she let him take all the pain and carry it himself.

"Cassie, please, talk to me, love."

"I'm fine. I'm fine, Gray," she said in a voice that was so hushed he struggled to catch the words. "You're wrong.

I'm fine. Just have Rob ready tomorrow, all right?'' And she quietly cut the connection.

''That was Mom, wasn't it?''

Gray blinked hard. He ran one hand over his face, then turned to meet his son.

''Yes, Rob, it was. She's gone home to see to the store. She wants me to pack you up so she can come get you tomorrow.''

''Are you gonna do that?''

They studied each other and Gray realized that Cassie had been wrong that first day he'd confronted her. He and his son really did look more alike than she thought. The boy staring back at him looked lost. And scared. And mad as hell, his stubborn chin jutting out.

''I'm going to pack your things.''

''But something's wrong with Mom. She wouldn't just go home like that without stopping by. She wouldn't.''

Gray closed his eyes, opened them, and looked his son steadily in the face. Man to man.

''You got me there, buddy. I agree with you one hundred percent. She wouldn't do that.''

''But you said you were packing my things. That means—we're going now, aren't we? We're going home together, right? Or don't you care about her? Doesn't it even bother you that something's wrong and she's alone?''

Only so much that he was about to ignore all the sane and wise things he knew he should pay attention to. So much that he couldn't think of anything but getting to her right now.

He turned to his child. ''I care, Rob. I love your mother heart and soul. Is that…all right with you? We talked about this once before. How do you feel about me loving your mom?''

Rob started breathing hard and fast. He rocked from one foot to the other. ''I feel good. I feel really good about that, but Mom—I'm not so sure how she feels right now.

I just wish you'd hurry and fix things up with her so that we can all be happy together."

Gray knelt by his son. "I want that, too. I wish I could do that. Make everything right with her, but your mom and I, we go way back. Lots of history. I'm not sure I can do that. Things aren't always that simple with grown-ups."

Fiddling with the buttons on his shirt, Rob nodded. "I know that. Like how you didn't know I was even yours. But what will happen if you can't make things right with Mom? What if things can't work? Will I still...will I still see you?"

He gazed up at Gray with those big, blue eyes framed by long dark lashes and Gray could see the tears he was fighting not to shed.

Gently he touched his child's cheek, cupping his jaw with one hand. "If your mom and I can't make things work, then I'll still see you when I can. And I'll still love both of you. That's all. I'll still love you. Always."

"Me, too. I will. I'll still love you no matter what, Dad," Rob said, launching himself into Gray's arms. His skinny little body shook with sobs, he wrapped his arms tightly around his father's neck and held on.

Gray hugged him close, ran his hand down the buttons of his spine.

"Come on, son. Let's go," he whispered against the soft, dark hair. "Let's get you home. Let's go see your mom."

But when they finally arrived at the house, there was no sign of life. The animals had been farmed out to friends, the store was already closed for the day. Gray's car sat in the drive, but Cassie was nowhere in sight.

Panic climbed into Gray's throat, and he fought it for his child's sake, but it was Rob who turned to him, calmer now. Old-man serious.

"Sometimes when she needs to think, she goes and sits

by that little pond on the back of Mr. Moser's property. He doesn't ever go there, and it's kind of quiet.''

''You think I'll find her there? You'll be okay here by yourself?''

''This is home, Dad,'' Rob said simply, and nodded his father toward the pond.

Gray watched while his son moved up onto the porch. Then he turned to walk away himself.

''Good luck, Dad,'' Rob said as Gray began what felt like the longest journey of his life. He knew that luck would not be enough today. Not nearly enough. There had to be more than that.

He skirted around the rows of trees, kept walking past the house, continued on until he saw her. She was kneeling by the water, trailing her fingers, staring at some distant point on the horizon.

When he drew closer, she looked up, stumbling in her haste to rise.

''Gray.'' Her voice was a painful whisper. Her eyes darted to the side.

''He's at the house.''

''I told you I'd come get him tomorrow.''

''I know that.'' He reached her side and tried to take her hand. She stepped back, slithered away.

''Cass, do you think I know you so little that I couldn't tell something was wrong? Did you honestly think I could have stayed in town worrying about you? What happened? What in hell did he say to you?''

She opened her mouth, then shut it again, shaking her head.

''Go home, Gray. I'll call you to work things out about Rob. Some other time. Not today. Please, not today.''

''What did he say to you? Whatever it was, I'm sorry. So damn sorry. I'm sorry for everything. I've done everything wrong with you right from the beginning. All of it. I'm sorry for that, too.''

"Gray, don't do this," she begged as he stepped closer. She sidestepped him again, the soft folds of her skirt swaying with her movement. "You don't have to apologize for anything. You didn't force me to make love to you that day. You didn't drag me into anything. And you don't owe me anything now. I'm a big girl, remember? I can take care of myself. I'm...fine. You shouldn't have come. Go home, please." And she raised her eyes to the sky, but he could see that misty tears filled them, blurring the sweet blue.

"I don't want to leave you like this. My father—"

"I don't want you to feel responsible for me. You don't have to." She was twisting the material of her skirt, but she still managed to look him in the eye. "And as for your father, I don't know what you heard, but I don't want your money, either."

"He tried to buy you."

"He thought I'd jump at the chance to marry into the Alexander fortune, but—I don't want your money, Gray."

"Sweetheart, don't you think I know that? Don't you think I know you, just a little?"

She had her arms wrapped around herself now and was shaking her head at him, her dark bangs feathering across her forehead. "I'd *never* marry for money. I never, ever, planned to marry you, no matter what."

Gray closed his eyes. He felt the pain zip through his body. Maybe she was right. Maybe in coming here, in refusing to leave, he was hurting her, but—

He took two steps forward, cupped her chin with his palm. "I know you don't want my money. I know you never planned to marry me. I've asked you to before and you've turned me down, but I'm asking again, Cass. Really asking from deep down inside. Marry me. Please."

"Because you feel you have a duty to me?"

He brushed his thumb across her lips and shook his head

slowly, holding her gaze. "No. Because I love you, sweetheart."

Her eyes widened, her chin trembled. "Don't say that. You don't mean it. You don't love me." She placed her fingers over his lips as if to stop his words, and he kissed them and gave them back to her.

"I love you," he repeated. "I didn't realize it was love. I didn't want it to be love, because you'd turned me away before. But every time I asked you to marry me, it killed me when you turned me down. The first time. Every time."

A tremulous smile formed on her lips, but she still didn't answer.

"I know you don't want my money, but I'm glad I have it if it means I can take better care of you and Rob. Don't hold it against me because I'm rich, or because you don't like my name, Cass. Love me back. Eleven years ago, you totally slayed me, sweetheart. You stole my heart, and I haven't gotten over you yet. I'm never going to get past loving you. You once told me I was the prince of Misunderstood. I don't know about that, but I know for sure that you're the princess of my dreams. You always have been, love."

He reached into his pocket, pulled out a box and flipped it open, revealing a small gold band.

"Rob helped me pick it out on the way over," he admitted sheepishly. "It's not a glass slipper, but it means the same thing. Do you think it will fit? Do you think I could fit—that you could ever someday feel that I could be someone you would want as a husband, as a lover?"

Cassie looked up into the eyes of the man she'd loved forever. He couldn't be saying these things. She shouldn't be listening, beginning to believe.

And yet she held out her hand. He slipped the ring on. It slid on easily, dangling a bit, clearly too big.

"I'm sorry. We were in a bit of a hurry," he explained,

his brows furrowing as he held her hand in his own. "I wanted it to be perfect for you."

"It is." She smiled up into his eyes and snaked one hand up around his neck. "It's a perfect fit. *You're* a perfect fit for me."

"Oh, love, I knew that. Why didn't you?" He laughed, gathered her arms behind his neck and kissed her. Slowly and thoroughly.

And for once Cassie stayed right where she was, close against Gray's heart.

"I loved you too much," she told him, rising on her toes to whisper against his mouth. "I was afraid to hope that two people from such different worlds could ever be together."

A low groan escaped him. "You couldn't love me too much."

"It felt that way. You were so handsome, so unattainable. I loved you from the beginning," she confessed. "And I just pretended to myself and you that I didn't care. Because I was afraid."

"Don't be afraid anymore, Cass," he pleaded, dropping kisses on her eyes, her nose, her lips. "And love me until the end."

"Even longer," she promised. "I will. I always will."

"And you'll marry me, in spite of my father and my money and any other differences you think we have."

"I'll definitely marry you. Because we share what's most important. I'll marry you. Not for duty or money, but for love and happiness."

"Say that again, my love," he urged, drawing her close.

"I'll marry you. My love."

Epilogue

It all looks so different,'' Cass said, staring out over the spot where Gray's trailer had sat the summer before.

Gray chuckled. ''That's what Mr. Moser said when he came by the other day.''

Cass shook her head and smiled at her husband. ''You two. He didn't convince you that you should have paid him more money just because you spruced up the orchard after he sold it to you, did he? You already gave him twice what the market value was.''

''But he looked so sad,'' Gray argued.

''Gray Alexander.''

She whooped when he picked her up and swung her around, finally setting her down when they were both disheveled and breathless. ''Cass, love, you don't have to worry. Mr. Moser didn't fleece me. He and I understand each other.''

She touched his cheek. ''I know. And it was nice of you to let him stay on at his house. He wouldn't admit it, but he gets lonely all on his own.''

Her husband took her fingers and kissed them one by

one. "Hmm, it was even nicer of you to invite my father over for dinner last week. No one would have blamed you if you had chosen to ignore him."

She shrugged. "He's your father, Gray, and he behaved himself for the most part. He and Malcolm even managed to find some common ground."

"You mean the fact that they both think we should start having more children right away?"

She smiled and cuddled closer to him. "You don't sound too disenchanted with the idea yourself."

"Wow, this is great," Rob said, coming up behind them. "Bailey's going to have lots of space to roam around in once everything's done."

Cass looked back to her former home. The frame was now twice the size it had been, and the smell of fresh-cut wood filled the air.

"Plenty of room for animals *and* babies," Rob said, looking up wistfully at his parents.

Gray hugged his wife, who was starting to chuckle. "We'll make some soon. Babies, that is," Gray promised.

Cass leaned back in Gray's arms. "Your childhood dream coming true," she said, indicating the orchard.

He rested his head on her hair. "Yes, but you and Rob are the greatest dream a man could have. A wife and son I love more than life."

She turned in his arms. "Mmm. I was just thinking the same thing. A son I adore and the man of my dreams right here beside me. It's heaven."

Rob rolled his eyes, and Cassie wrinkled her nose at her son.

"Well, it is," she said. Gray grinned down at his son.

"Better look away if you don't want to see your parents acting like teenagers, Rob."

Shaking his head, Rob studied his parents and smiled.

"Well, aren't you going to kiss her again?" he finally asked.

"And again and again," Gray promised as he laid his lips on his wife's and a thousand dreams came true.

* * * * *

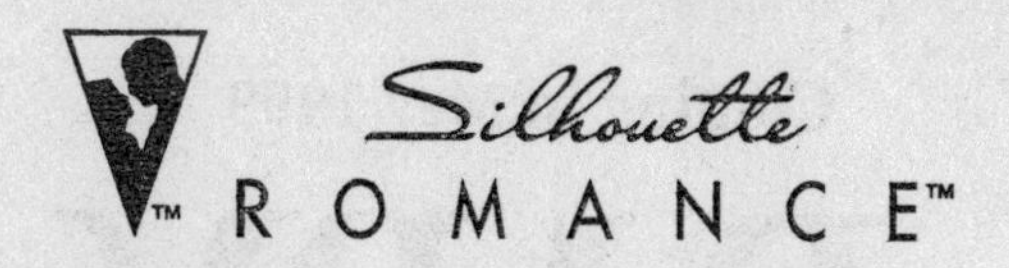

COMING NEXT MONTH

#1366 THE MARRIAGE MERGER—Vivian Leiber
Loving the Boss
Prim-and-proper assistant Patricia Peel had secretly dreamed of becoming her handsome boss's wife. So when Sam Wainwright proposed, she said yes. Of course it was only a *pretend* engagement, but Patricia was determined to turn it into a very *real* marriage....

#1367 THE BABY ARRANGEMENT—Moyra Tarling
Bundles of Joy
He had been searching high and low for his son, so when Jared McAndrew discovered Faith Nelson with his child, he naturally demanded she come home with him. So how could Faith convince Jared that he'd found the wrong twin—but the right bride?

#1368 MILLIONAIRE ON HER DOORSTEP—Stella Bagwell
Twins on the Doorstep
Dashing executive Adam Murdock Sanders had promised that he would never allow himself to be hurt by love again. But one look at Maureen York, and he knew his promise was in danger of being broken. Because Maureen tempted a man to dream of all sorts of things—kisses, long embraces...wedding bells....

#1369 FAIRY-TALE FAMILY—Pat Montana
When prodigal son Mitch Kole returned home to take care of his father, he ran smack into Ellie Sander and her small family. Mitch never thought he was daddy material until Ellie showed him that daddies—and husbands—come in all shapes and sizes....

#1370 THE TRIPLET'S WEDDING WISH—DeAnna Talcott
She had always had a crush on Jack Conroy, so when he kissed her, Abigail was thrilled—until he mistook her for her triplet sister. Now Abigail must show Jack that the sister who was always perfect for him had been under his nose the whole time!

#1371 NEVADA COWBOY DAD—Dorsey Kelley
Family Matters
Rusty Sheffield knew that the only place to raise his baby niece was at the Lazy S Ranch—but soon found out he only owned half the ranch. Still one look at Lucy Donovan had Rusty determined to lay claim to his land—and the tempestuous beauty who came with it.